~ The Disappea

Destiny Falls M

By Elizabeth Pantley

www.NoCrySolution.com
© Elizabeth Pantley, Better Beginnings, Inc. 2021
With special thanks to Robert and Linda
Cover Design by Molly Burton, Cozy Cover Designs
https://cozycoverdesigns.com/
Editing by Melissa Bowersock

Disclaimer

This book is a work of fiction. Names, characters, places, and incidents are products of the author's imagination. Any resemblance to actual people, living or dead, or actual places or events is purely coincidental.

Table of Contents

1

The mountain trail was tricky. I was moving slowly through the deep snow. I knew the lake had to be nearby. It was important to find it, but I could barely see ten feet in front of me due to the storm. The trail was steep and slippery, and I was making my way using trekking poles to assess where I should step next. My hands and feet were cold. I heard Latifa calling out to me. Where was she? What was she saying?

"Good morning, Sunshine!" Her lilting voice woke me from my dream. *"Happy one-month-a-versary!"*

It's amazing how accustomed I'd grown to my cat's telepathic voice in my head. I squinted at my fluffy Himalayan sidekick. She was sitting beside me on the bed. I stretched out my arms and gave an extra-loud yawn in her direction, hoping she'd get the hint that she had woken me up.

"Message received. Woke you up. So sorry. Got it." She squinted at me and whispered, *"Not sorry."*

I yawned at her again.

"Bet you forgot today is one month from the earth-shattering day we arrived in Destiny Falls." Her big, baby blues were focused on me, and her whiskers were twitching. *"I have appointed myself Keeper of Your Calendar. You can be so forgetful*

about celebratory dates." She shook her furry head as if it were impossible to believe.

I gave another exaggerated stretch and reached over to the bedside table. With a flourish, I presented her with a small, gift-wrapped package.

"*Squeeee! You remembered!*" She head-butted my face and spun a little circle on the bed, then turned to tear open the package. There was more squealing as she discovered her new, feathered cat toy.

I patted my sidekick's head and tossed my legs over the side of the bed. A glance at my phone confirmed that Latifa-the-alarm-clock was right on time. I needed to get changed and meet Axel downstairs for a morning jog into town. He was often too busy with work to join me in the morning, so it was a wonderful treat to have some extra time with my newfound brother.

My brother. How I loved the sound of that. After a lifetime as an only child in a tiny three-person family, finding out that I had siblings and a large hidden family was monumental. Add to that a mysterious, magical new world, and I was floating on cloud nine.

The only dark spot was missing my family and my best friend, Luna. I was still trying to figure out how to tell them about Destiny Falls. I'd have to sort this out soon, since my cover story of a working trip to Denmark was nearing its expiration. A month overseas was feasible, but as the timeline continued, I'd need to address my disappearance.

My Nana and Granana would be happy that I was happy. They'd been my biggest cheerleaders my entire life. They always said my happiness mattered most to them. Both my parents disappeared the week I was born, so my grandmother and great-grandmother jumped into raising me. They were dedicated to the job, with an enthusiasm that was a complete contrast to their tiny, delicate appearances. Luna and I referred to them as the Mighty Minis, which was an apt description.

Figuring out how to explain that I wasn't really in Denmark, but in a magical, hidden town in an unknown location was a whole new ball of wax. Especially since the town was finicky about who it revealed itself to. Any e-mails or texts I attempted to send explaining my location, disappeared into the ether in a wisp of bounces—undeliverable, message not sent, connection lost. Even phone calls suddenly lost the signal. Maybe Axel, my brother—deep sigh of joy—could help me solve this problem.

I turned on the movie channel for Latifa, my furry little movie buff, tucked my ponytail through the back of my baseball cap, and headed out. I strolled slowly down the hallway, so I could absorb the beauty of this amazing home.

Hmm. That was odd. Where was the window seat? It was usually somewhere in my hallway, but it was oddly absent. There was a glorious swatch of sunlight, which is where it normally would be lounging. I snickered. Imagine that. A window seat that could lounge in the sun. Magic touched the Caldwell Crest home in the most interesting ways.

Caldwell Crest was a masterpiece of design. It could be described as a cozy, mansion-sized mountain cabin. I felt embraced by the sweeping staircase made of polished wood. I loved the plank wood floors and ceilings and the gorgeous but understated chandeliers. I adored the stone fireplaces that soared all the way up to the tall ceiling. The earthy colors of the décor were soothing. Even after a month, I was still adjusting to the fact that it was now where I lived.

The home was enchanting. I could have almost believed the rumors that it was originally built as a castle back in the 1800s and magically remodeled many times. It was difficult to understand Caldwell Crest and the mysterious place that was Destiny Falls, especially since the definition seemed to always be changing.

It had been a wild ride of a month since I'd been thrown through a portal and landed here.

Destiny Falls was different from any place I'd ever known before. I had to let go of my preconceived notions of what defines a town. I still couldn't quite wrap my head around the fact that the town wasn't on any map and wasn't accessible by normal means.

I still don't understand it all, but I know that a person must be called here by either the home or the town. Then they whoosh through time and space, to the accompaniment of a flash of brilliant light, as they tumble through a mirror—as I did. It's a one-way trip. Once you're here, you are, well . . . "trapped" is a harsh word for such a lovely place. However, it was accurate. I could not choose to leave. Destiny Falls controlled the comings and goings.

I felt a bit like Alice falling through the mirror into wonderland. Albeit a much nicer wonderland than Alice had to deal with.

I'd figured out that it was easier if I just went with the flow and didn't try to understand all the nuances of this place.

It was time to get moving and meet up with my brother Axel. I loved the sound of that. I'd been an only child all my life, and now all I wanted to say was *brother, brother, brother*.

As I stepped into the most beautiful kitchen of all time, I looked around to see what was new. Some days, it was the same as before, but on others, I would find something entirely different. A breakfast nook would appear where just a window was located before. On another day, the nook would transition into a large, formal dining room.

I took a deep breath and absorbed the glorious, homey feeling that enveloped me. The wood cabinets gleamed like they'd just been polished. The acres of black marble countertops reflected the twinkling lights. The collection of pretty copper pots hung on a rack suspended on long, black wires from the ceiling high above me. The cabinlike wood walls finished off the feel of a warm, rustic retreat.

I was so busy absorbing my surroundings that I didn't even see Axel enter the room.

"Good morning, Hayden!" He pulled me in for a hug and finished it with a friendly tap on the bill of my hat. "Ready for a run or do you want a cup of tea first?"

"Oh, tea, please!" I noticed that he already had the tea fixings set up in the breakfast nook, along with a platter of rolls and fruit. I was moved that he already knew my routine and went through this effort.

"Did you give Princess Latifa her one-month-a-versary present?"

"I did! She's up there now, batting it around and watching a movie. I expect I'll find Chanel up there when I return. You know, she still won't tell me how the two of them get in and out of the bedrooms. She's afraid I'll put the kibosh on her freedom if I know the secret."

"She's not wrong there," Axel said. "You tend to be a helicopter fur mother. Is that a thing? Fur mother? I've heard the fur baby phrase."

"Yeah, that's hilarious," I said. "But, you're not wrong. I'm an overprotective fur momma. Guilty as charged."

Bright morning sunlight flooded the cheery lime green and white breakfast nook. Looking out the wall of windows, I could see a group of sailboats racing in front of us. As I sat down, I looked to my left and noticed that the window seat was located right beside the nook, with a pretty, white Persian cat asleep on the pillow.

"Ah, there's Chanel. And that's where the window seat ended up this morning! I've never seen it downstairs before."

Axel nodded as he reached for a breakfast roll. "There's a first time for everything."

2

"I have a treat planned for you this morning," Axel said as we headed out the door. "Two surprising places to visit. It's about a forty-five-minute run to get there, but usually only about fifteen minutes to get home."

He said that with such nonchalance—as if the surprise were at the end of the run, not the fact that the distance was variable. I was still adjusting to the unique magic of Destiny Falls, and it never ceased to amaze me. But now, instead of being shocked, I was charmed.

"What's the surprise?" I asked.

"Oh, you're one of *those*." Axel nodded his head.

"One of what?"

"Those people who spoil surprises by finding out about them in advance. I bet you peek at your Christmas gifts and read spoilers in book reviews, too." He shuddered and shook his head. "So sad."

"I'd like to be offended, but it's true. I sometimes read the last page of a book before I start it."

His eyes popped open wide, and he gasped, "You do what?!"

"Well, it makes perfect sense," I said. "I like happy endings, and I hate when things end badly for characters I've grown to love. So, unless I'm certain a book has a HEA, I'll peek at the last page."

"HEA?" he asked.

"Happily Ever After."

"Okay, Cinderella. I'm only going to tell you we're heading to my friend Vessie's coffee shop, and to check in on a new tenant. You'll love to see both, so there's no need to peek at the ending."

"Ha. Ha. Ha."

He took off running down the driveway and yelled, "Come on, slowpoke!"

The morning was typical for Destiny Falls, at least since the day I'd arrived. Warm and sunny with a bright blue sky and a scattering of puffy white clouds. A gentle breeze was just enough to pleasantly balance the warm temperature.

Flowers lined the driveway and the entry to West Caldwell Lane. There was a different arrangement of flowers there every day. They always grew in happy abundance. Today, the flowers were in every shade of purple. There was a trellis leading out to the main road that was lush with purple, hanging wisteria vines highlighted with white climbing roses. Of course, there was no way that the flowers were dug up and replanted every day, so I accepted it as one of the enchanted features of Caldwell Crest.

We ran down the street and turned the corner to Twin Falls Park Road. My new friend Olivia was walking out to her mailbox. Her gorgeous dog, Hercules, was beside her as usual.

"Good morning!" She waved and smiled.

We slowed to a stop in front of her home, and Hercules walked over to me. "Hi there, big boy." I reached out to pet his soft fur. As usual, he leaned his body into mine and relaxed into being petted. He was a Saarloos wolfdog, a mix of a German shepherd and a grey wolf, and was the largest canine I'd ever known. He was an amazing protection dog, and on more than one occasion had been my own personal sentry and rescuer. I always carried a bag of meat in my backpack when I ran this route, as an ongoing thank you to him for being my protector. I held out a handful of his snack, and he gobbled it up as we chatted with Olivia. As usual, she was a fount of information about the community. It was impossible to keep a secret from this one.

"Did you tell Hayden who took over the DF Camping & Hunting store?" she asked Axel. She was bouncing in place, barely able to contain the gossip.

"Actually, we're headed there now." He tilted his head toward me, and shrugged his shoulders, subtly trying to stop her from spilling the beans. "It was going to be a surprise."

"Oops!" Olivia said, totally missing his signals. Or intentionally missing them, so she could provide the news. It was one of her favorite things to do. "Hayden, you're never going to guess who it is!"

As always, there was no point in guessing.

She'd jump right in to tell me if I paused for a breath. "Gwendolyn broke the lease on her shop. She never really wanted it. It was just a way to get back at her ex-husband, winning it in the divorce, you know. That woman hated her ex as much as she hated anything to do with camping and . . ."

"Who took over the store?" I gently interrupted to get her back on track. I wanted her to say it before Axel stopped her from giving me the name.

"Oh! Right. You really need to meet her; she's a hoot. Her name is Poppy and get this! She's Cleobella's sister!" Olivia looked at me with wide eyes and clapped her hands enthusiastically.

Cleobella was my grandmother Caldwell's personal assistant, housekeeper, and all-around support person. She was one of the most unique people I'd ever met. She silently appeared at my grandmother's side whenever there was something to be done or food to be served, gliding in and out of rooms at precisely the right time with whatever Grandmother needed. I had yet to figure out their system of communication, but I felt it would be rude to ask.

Before I first saw her in person, I had seen evidence of her stealthy helpfulness. I had expected that she was an unobtrusive, blend-into-the-background, grey-dress-with-a-white apron kind of person. I was very, very wrong. *Very* wrong.

Cleobella was a tall, elegant woman with the most striking white-blond, waist-length hair.

Every time I saw her, it was done up in some elaborate fashion, and often topped with a glamourous hat. No bland, grey uniform for this woman. She dressed like a cross between Cher and Lady Gaga in full costume, from her fancy hat to her usually sky-high heels. She was dressed up like this no matter what the day or the task. I could find her cleaning the kitchen in full-on Gaga.

Cleobella was deaf and couldn't speak, but her presence was anything but silent. She seemed to fill a room with her extraordinary appearance. I was wondering if her sister was anything like her when Olivia answered that question.

"You think Cleobella is unique? Her sister is cut from the same cloth. They're two of a kind. And wait until you see the store! It's spectacular! Seriously, Hayden—go see the shop and meet Poppy."

I could barely hear Axel murmuring under his breath, "That was the plan."

Axel said we'd meet Poppy first since it was on our route to the coffee shop. When we walked up to the DF Camping & Hunting Store, I got the shivers, remembering how completely horrible Gwendolyn was. She was haggard and bad-tempered, and that was just her outward appearance. Deep down she was downright evil, and I'd had a frightening encounter with her. Thankfully, she was gone now.

I noticed the shop's sign had changed. It now read *Poppy's Camping & Hiking Extravaganza*. I stepped inside the store ahead of Axel and stopped dead in my tracks, frozen by shock and awe. The entire store looked vastly different from the last time we were here when it had looked like a typical sporting goods store.

This shop was no longer typical in any way. It was set up like a campground and hiking trail. *Exactly* like a campground and hiking trail. I could have sworn I was outdoors. I looked way up through enormous trees to what was painted to look like a blue sky. I felt like dipping my toes into the babbling brook that wound its way through the center of the store. I felt like roasting a marshmallow at one of the various campsites that were set up. Everything I could possibly need for a first-class camping trip was displayed in a real-life setting.

There was no reasonable way that all this would fit into a building this size, and I was giddy with the idea that Destiny Falls made such magic happen.

I spotted a tall woman with white-blond hair near the edge of a display area. It had to be Poppy.

"There she is," Axel said as he raised his hand to wave.

We made our way over a small wooden bridge that crossed the brook, and Axel called out to her. She waved back merrily with both arms. As she rounded the corner and made her way toward us, I got my first eyeful of Cleobella's sister. Clearly, they shared wardrobe and makeup tips.

Poppy would have fit right in with a Cirque du Soleil performance if they had a show with an enchanted wilderness theme. She could have been an overgrown woodland fairy in her green floral dress, lacy tights, and wispy vest made of delicate green lace. Her gorgeous hair was braided together with flowers and it flowed down her back. She was wearing theatre-style makeup, with her eye shadow in a colorful rainbow palate to match her outfit. It was obvious she and Cleobella bought their fake eyelashes in the same place. The lashes were like two glamorous spiders framing her colorful eye makeup. Just like her sister, it was impossible to determine her age. She could have been thirty, sixty, or anything in between.

Poppy's well-worn hiking boots, with grey wool socks peeking out from over the tops, were a charmingly appropriate touch. She skipped forward—yes, skipped! —her dimples in full display as she smiled brightly. I loved Poppy before she said a single word.

"Hi, Axel!" she sang out in a sweet, melodic voice.

"Hi, Poppy. I want you to meet my sister, Hayden. The store is dynamic! I couldn't wait to show her."

"So happy to meet you, Hayden. Eleanor has told me so much about you."

I glanced at Axel. I had no idea that my grandmother knew Cleobella's family, though it made perfect sense since they had worked closely together for years.

Poppy did a little spin on her boot-clad toes and opened her arms wide, gesturing to her new store. "Move-in is almost complete!" she said.

Axel and I both enthused over the real-life camping experience. This caused Poppy to blush happily.

"It's amazing that you fit all of this inside the shop," I said.

Poppy's dimples came back in full display. "Oh, I wish. But that's not how it works. Destiny Falls decided that more locals need to partake of our wonderful parks and trails. So, it seemed that a store to help them prepare was needed. I'm just the gatekeeper, so to speak. I was as surprised as you are by all this!"

She spent a few minutes showing us around the various features, my favorite being the enormous mountain-like climbing wall topped with snow.

As soon as we were outside, Axel turned to me. "I knew you'd love Poppy. Isn't her store amazing? You can't see it all at once. We'll need to come back."

"Oh, yes, please," I said. "Every time I think I've hit the pinnacle of Destiny Falls' enchantments I see a new delight."

"Yep. Never a dull moment. Ready for another fun stop? I want to take you to meet Vessie and see her coffee shop. It's just a few blocks' walk from here, and we can grab an early lunch if you'd like."

"I'd love to!" Now that my imagination was stirred, I was ready for more hidden treasures.

We made our way down the street while chatting about anything and everything. Axel managed the Caldwell's many properties here, including the building that housed Poppy's new shop. He knew everyone in town, so he regaled me with stories and interesting tidbits about the places and people of Destiny Falls. I so enjoyed spending time with my *brother*—yes, I said it again-—and was feeling more at home as the weeks passed.

3

We rounded the corner, and I scanned the waterfront road ahead. The ferry took up the entire block, except for a small ice cream stand near the ferry entrance. The boat was docked, so I got my first close-up look at it. It was far more beautiful than any ferry I'd ever ridden. Painted in navy blue and white, it had small white lights that highlighted the entire length of the vessel, and a group of flags fluttered on the top. It resembled a yacht more than a working boat.

The row of shops that lined the street across from the ferry would appeal to travelers. Souvenir shops, clothing boutiques, art galleries, and restaurants made it a welcoming harbor.

A man came off the ferry and smiled and raised his arm to wave at us, but then he looked confused and dropped his arm. I looked behind me to see if he was gesturing to someone else, but I didn't see anyone there.

What I saw, on a slight hill just across from the ferry, was a brilliant pink and white striped awning that stood out from all the rest like a shining beacon. As it turned out, we were headed directly toward the pink beacon. The sign above the door read *Vessie's Hideaway Café*.

Axel opened the door, and we stepped into the pinkest place I'd ever seen. If Christmas and the Fourth of July had a pink baby, this shop would be it. The walls—pink. Ceiling—pink. Furniture—pink. The floor had a dash of gray but was predominately pink. The room was not just pink! It was a luminous pink that almost made the air glow.

Flowing lines of butterflies, in colors from bubblegum to magenta, decorated the walls. They fluttered almost as if they were alive. The ceiling was painted to resemble a sunset, a swirling blend of the subtlest pastel pinks and cream.

There was an eating bar with upholstered stools made of pink leather, tufted with large white buttons. A collection of tables filled the center of the room. Their white tops were decorated with a pattern of artistically scattered pink and purple. Flamingo-pink chairs completed the eating area.

In one corner was a children's area made to look like Cinderella's coach. It was filled with toys and games. It seemed like a great place for kids to play while their parents enjoyed coffee or a meal.

All that pink should have been a bit overwhelming, but the overall effect was surprisingly wonderful.

A woman came out from behind the counter, heading toward us with a welcoming smile. She was wearing . . . not pink, but a striking purple summer dress. She had artful highlights of purple in her hair. She was a bright spot of color that blended beautifully with her surroundings.

"Axel, hi!" She gave him a quick hug and turned to me. "This must be Hayden! Hi, I'm Vessie. Welcome to my pink paradise."

I reached out to shake her hand, but she bypassed it and hugged me. "I'm delighted to meet you. Happy that this knucklehead finally brought you by!" She playfully poked him in the arm, and he rubbed it with an exaggerated 'ouch.' They both laughed. I liked her immediately.

"Grab a seat." She pointed. The place was packed, and we settled at one of the few empty tables.

"Can you stay for something to eat?" she asked.

"That's the plan," said Axel. "I was hoping you'd be able to join us for a bit."

"Can do!" she said. "Let me touch base with the kitchen and I'll be right back."

We sat down and I noticed the man at the next table was staring at me. When I caught his eye, he didn't look embarrassed; instead, he winked, smiled, and gave me a salute. He was quite a character. Tall and thin, he wore black glasses, a bow tie, and a handlebar mustache. When he smiled, one gold front tooth was on display. Who on earth—besides rappers—had a gold tooth? He continued to watch me while I settled in my seat. My eyes darted around the room in discomfort. Finally, he looked away and returned to his meal.

Vessie returned to our table bearing cups of the most delicious, creamy chai. A server brought four platters brimming with an assortment of menu tastings.

"I wanted to give you a bit of everything," she said. "Don't expect a platter every time you come in, though."

"Oh, darn." Axel rubbed his hands together. "I was hoping this was your new special."

The three of us had a marvelous time, enjoying the food and our visit. I had the feeling right off that Vessie belonged in my life.

After our feast and visit ended, Vessie walked us to the door and invited me to drop by anytime. I told her I'd make her café a regular stop after my morning run, and she seemed pleased by that.

Axel and I stepped outside just as passengers were coming off the mystery ferry. Signs did not show the ferry's routes, and any maps I found seemed to be intentionally vague. Whenever I asked anyone about it, I got confusing answers. People would say things like, "It depends on your destination," or, "Routes change depending on the passengers." The clandestine attitude was par for the course here in Destiny Falls. I would keep pressing until I got answers.

We sat on a bench in front of Vessie's to people-watch, chat, and enjoy the water view before we headed back home.

A group of women was standing in front of the ferry landing. They were looking at us and whispering to each other. I glanced around, but we were the only people there, so they were looking at me or Axel. I looked back at them, and they looked away. Perhaps it was just seeing a new person in a small town, so I said nothing to Axel, but I decided to be alert to any other odd behavior from the residents of this puzzling community.

4

The sunrise was casting a glow over my room. I gently shifted two sleeping cats away from me. Chanel had started sneaking in here during the middle of the night. Latifa told me she had bad dreams, so there was no way I'd ban her from climbing into bed with us. Although it got a bit squished with two big furballs who gravitated toward the warm human.

I snuck out of bed, changed into my running clothes, and quietly left the room. I relished my quiet morning jogs when few people were out and about. It started my day right. I knew that Vessie would be opening by the time I got there, and I was looking forward to seeing her again, and enjoying a cup of tea and breakfast in her charming café. This could quickly become a morning ritual.

I opened the door to Vessie's pinker-than-pink café. The butterflies on the walls today were making their way around the room, their wings fluttering gently. The air in the café seemed to reflect the warm glow of the sunrise.

Vessie was making a pot of coffee. She waved over at me and pointed to the coffeemaker. I gave her a thumbs-up, then approached the counter where a man and woman were standing, likely waiting for their coffee. I smiled and said good morning.

They were both wearing uniforms bearing a logo that matched the one I'd seen on the ferry sign. The woman's name tag read *Captain*. I asked if she was the one who drove the ferry.

"Nope, I'm the one who manages the crew and oversees the voyage." She gestured toward the man next to her. "Allow me to introduce our helmsman, the man who drives the ferry."

The man gave a slight bow. "Kerbie Gomez at your service, ma'am." He reached up to shake my hand. He was shorter than my great-grandmother, five-feet tall on her tiptoes. He was about as wide as he was tall and had the brightest red hair I'd ever seen.

"Nice to meet you," I said.

"Likewise," he croaked in a very deep, gravelly voice, the opposite of what I had expected from his appearance.

"I'm Nakita." The captain held out her hand to shake. She was staring intently into my eyes, which made me just a touch uncomfortable. "You must be new here. I don't think I've seen you before."

"You're right, I'm new. Nice to meet you, Nakita," I said. "I'm Hayden Caldwell. I really enjoy watching your ferry activity."

Vessie walked up to the counter. "Hi Nakita. Kerbie. Coffee's brewing. Good morning, Hayden! What can I get you? Chai tea? I have oatmeal with caramelized bananas and pecans today, or blueberry waffles?"

"Tea and oatmeal sound delicious," I said.

Vessie turned back toward the kitchen, and I excused myself and walked down the long hallway to the bathrooms. As I made my way down the hall, I heard footsteps behind me. I turned to see Nakita right behind me. She gestured me to the farthest corner, past the restroom doors. She had an apprehensive look on her face. It made me a little uneasy, and I couldn't imagine what she wanted.

She whispered in a voice so quiet I could barely hear her and, while she talked, she kept glancing down the hallway.

"Miss Caldwell, I can't believe you're here!" She glanced again down the hall as if looking for someone. "I'm sorry I couldn't help her. Maybe you can."

"What? Who?" I was so confused that I could not even formulate a decent question.

"I can't say more now." She looked again toward the front of the café. "Come to the ferry terminal day after tomorrow. Early. Before the gates open. There shouldn't be people around. If anyone sees you—leave."

"Come to the terminal?" I was trying to make sense of her whispers.

"If the area is clear, come to the backdoor. I'll be there. I have something I must give you. I'll explain everything to you then." She took one step toward the front and peered at the door again.

"Do not tell anyone about this. Come alone. You can trust no one! No one! Please be careful. For your safety. And for the safety of your entire family."

"I don't understand," I said.

"If they know we spoke, we'll all be in danger."

"Who?" I asked her.

Just then, the bells on the front door jangled, and two tall, hefty men in greasy-looking ferry uniforms came into the café. Possibly mechanics. They approached the counter, and I heard them talking to Kerbie and ordering coffee.

Nakita reached out and grabbed my shoulders and shook me. She looked at me with the most desperate, pleading look in her eyes. "Please. Come to the terminal," she said again. "It's life or death. Tell no one."

The ferry captain reached around me and opened the restroom door. She was still talking to me, but since she was whispering and pushing me into the bathroom, I couldn't hear her. It sounded like she said 'never' and 'Gladstone' and 'danger.'

"Gladstone?" I asked. "Is that a person or a place?"

She put her finger to her mouth in the universal sign for shushing and shut the bathroom door behind me.

I opened the door and peeked out. She wildly shook her head signaling no and shoved me back into the restroom.

I stood inside the restroom, stunned. I could hear footsteps as she walked away. What in the world was that about? Clearly, she didn't want anyone to hear us, and she didn't want those two men to see us talking. Her tense demeanor and her message were disturbing. Life or death? Who even says that?

I had so many questions about the ferry. It had been a puzzling mystery to me since I'd arrived. No one would give me any straight answers about the ferry routes, and no books, maps, or signs provided straightforward information. Now I was being invited to meet with the captain at the ferry terminal. But under very unusual and disturbing conditions.

By the time I finished in the restroom, the captain, the helmsmen, and the two other ferry workers had left. Vessie had my tea and oatmeal ready and set up at the table in front of the window. She was waiting on another customer, so I took a seat.

While sipping my chai, I looked out the window at the ferry. They were just loading the morning travelers. People looked normal with their backpacks and rolling suitcases. A line of cars was slowly moving forward and funneling onto the boat. It all seemed so normal. But it wasn't, was it? Something very weird was going on.

"Good morning!" Vessie gave me a hug, then

took the seat across from me. "Enjoying the view?"

"I love it," I said. "You have the best spot in town. Being on the hill overlooking the harbor, you can see just about everything. And it's fun to watch the ferry come and go." I tried to sound nonchalant as I asked, "Where is the ferry going this morning?"

"Hmmm. Have no idea," she said. "It's different every day."

"Right. I've heard that. But it must have regular routes?"

"A few, I guess."

Geeze. This was like pulling teeth! Everyone in this town was so secretive about the ferry. It made my encounter with the captain that much more suspicious. But it made me more curious, too.

Vessie stood up. "Oops, my cakes are done. Let me run back and check them. Be right back."

Her cakes. Ha, sure! It was clear she was avoiding my question. It would be better if I knew more about the ferry before meeting the captain, right? I thought I'd make a stop at Olivia's on my way home. She knew just about everything about Destiny Falls, and she loved to talk. Maybe she could shed some light on this for me.

As I approached Olivia's home, Hercules came bounding down the stairs and ran over to meet me. He had the longest legs, so when he jumped or ran, he reminded me of a deer. A big, scary deer, with enormous teeth and whip-fast reflexes. Luckily, I was on his friend list. I didn't want to be this guy's enemy.

A minute later, Olivia came out her door and waved happily. She enjoyed company and was always up for a chat. Typically, if I warmed her up on a topic, she'd take it away and blabber about everything she knew until I stopped her or until she ran out of topic.

As always, she offered to bring out cookies and lemonade. Even though I had just left the café, I knew that serving visitors was a joyful treat for her, so I agreed. Plus, she made the best cookies.

I took a seat on the deck and enjoyed the view of the park just across the street. My buddy Hercules sat next to me. I stroked his soft fur while he laid his big, wolf-like head on my lap, his tongue hanging out like a puppy.

"Perfect timing, Hayden. I just made a fresh batch of sour cream snickerdoodles. You like those, yes?"

"I've never had them, but they sound amazing. I'm always up for a new cookie." I filled my plate and accepted a glass of lemonade.

"I was just in town at Vessie's, watching the ferry load up." Might as well dive right in, I thought.

"The Hideaway Café is the best place for ferry and people watching," said Olivia. "I've spent many hours there over the years."

"Have you ever been on the ferry? Where does it go?" I asked.

"Various islands around here," she said.

"What islands would those be?"

"Hmm. It's been a while, and they may have changed, and the routes change too." She tapped her chin with her finger. "There's quite a cluster of islands around us. Some of the small islands are privately owned, so I don't know their names. You need reservations well in advance. Even then, you might not get on. Tickets are hard to come by. It's a selective process."

She still wasn't giving me any names, which, for Olivia the chatterbox, seemed out of character.

"What about Gladstone?" I asked. "Is that one of them?"

She looked up, startled. "It's better if you don't speak of Gladstone."

"Why?" I asked.

"It's forbidden to travel there, and better that you don't even discuss it."

But she said it in a halting voice like she really wanted to say more. Then she shook her head. "Hmmm. No. Probably not something we should talk about. More lemonade?"

Olivia loved to talk, and she loved to share new information, so it was disconcerting that Gladstone was a topic she wanted to avoid. Yet another person being vague about the ferry and changing the topic. I knew I should let it go, but now I was more curious than ever. It made me decide to meet with Nakita. What better place for information about the ferry than the captain herself? I was looking forward to it.

I spotted a photo album on the table, and I gestured to it.

"Have you been reminiscing?" I asked Olivia.

"I have. No sense in having photo albums if you never look at them, right?" She stood up and brought it over to the table and pulled up a chair next to me. "Want to take a peek?"

She opened it up, and we flipped through the pages. There were many of her dog, of course. And lots of Twin Falls Park across the street from her home, the lake, and the one waterfall that most people saw.

I was one of the rare, lucky few who got a glimpse of the usually hidden second falls. It was enchanted and it offered me a glimpse of my future. I thought. As of now, I hadn't been able to uncover any information to verify this, but that's what it seemed to be.

In the vision, I saw myself as a mother with two young children and a man approaching us. Sadly, I'd had a bit of a mishap and didn't get to inspect the vision. But the man I saw was wearing a hiking backpack, with two trekking poles attached to the side. He was wearing a hat, and I think he had sunglasses on, but I couldn't be sure. It gave me goosebumps, and I wondered if the enigmatic vision was really telling my future. It seemed as if the experience was a rare one, and I'd yet to hear anyone else talk about it, so I kept quiet on the subject.

As I flipped to the next page, I gasped. It was a photo of my brother's friend, the town sheriff, Jaxson Redford. Oooo, he was a dreamboat! I didn't know if people still used that word, but, man, oh, man, it fit this guy. He was tall, with an athletic frame, a smooth, deep voice, and a sexy smile. And even better, he was smart and polite. There were some sparks between us I had yet to pursue since I hadn't been sure how long I'd be in Destiny Falls. Plus, we'd been involved in solving a murder to-gether. I'd rather have blocked out that memory.

Anyhow, the photo was of Jaxson. Standing on a trail in the park. He was carrying a hiking pack, with two trekking poles on the side. He was wearing a hat and sunglasses and smiling into the camera. He looked suspiciously like the man in my vision.

"How long ago was this taken?" I asked Olivia.

"Oh, maybe a year or so. I've known Jax since he was a tot, and once in a while he joins us on a hike."

I knew by "'us" she meant her and Hercules. I looked at the photo for a few minutes and won-dered. Was this *him*? Was Jaxson my destiny? Oh, now that inspired me to pursue those sparks to see where they led. Especially since it appeared I was here to stay in Destiny Falls.

Olivia and I finished up looking through the photo album. I helped her clean up the dishes from our cookies and lemonade. Then we had our goodbye hug, and I walked towards home. I needed some time to think.

I pondered the Destiny Falls ferry and my instructions from Nakita. Wild horses wouldn't keep me away from that appointment now. If I were wise, I'd bring someone with me. But she said, 'Tell no one.' Nakita specifically said it was 'life or death.' I would have to think this through before I told anyone about our encounter. The day after tomorrow. I'd be cautious, but it would be my opportunity to learn more.

Then I thought about the peek at my destiny and the photo of Jaxson. If he was the mystery man, that would be great, since he was one of my brother's best friends. I could imagine us together, blending into the Caldwell family with our two little children. The four of us hiking and camping together. Was he my future? If he was, there was no reason to rush it, but I wanted to spend more time with him to determine if we were the match that the falls predicted.

I continued my walk, pondering my possible future. As I walked past the hiking trailhead, a man was coming out of the woods to the parking area.

He was carrying a hiking backpack, with

two trekking poles attached to the side. He was wearing a hat and sunglasses. He also had the same build as the man I'd seen. Hmm. Okay, then. So much for Jaxson being the only one to fit the vision.

As he came closer, I realized the man ahead of me was none other than Han Chow.

Was he another possibility of my foretold future? I hoped so. He was special, and I was drawn to him. Han was a close Caldwell family friend and an investigator who helped solve the murder a few weeks ago. I was always comfortable with Han, and that was such a pleasant change, as usually I felt awkward around new guys. But Han was warm and easy to be around. He was a funny, clever, interesting guy. And oh my. Handsome. He reminded me of Henry Golding, the British actor from *Crazy Rich Asians* who also played Tom, the dreamy lead in the romantic comedy *Last Christmas*. Except he was an edgy, James Bond-ish version of the actor, but with the same wide, sexy smile and easygoing appeal.

As I walked his way, I spotted two other guys unloading their cars for a hike. They *both* were putting on hiking backpacks with trekking poles, and they both had on hats and sunglasses.

I laughed at myself. So much for figuring out the future father of my future children.

Han approached just then. "What's so funny, Hayden? Inside joke?"

"Was just thinking of something I saw. How

are you, Han?"

"Happy, but tired. Just finished a hike up to the falls. Ever been up there?"

Funny he should ask. "Yes, I have! It's one of the most beautiful places I've ever seen. Maybe even *the* most beautiful. I've hiked up there with Olivia a few times. It's a challenging hike, but so worth it."

"Agree," he said. "What are you up to today?"

"I was in town at Vessie's café, and then hung out with Olivia. My day got away from me, and I'm finally heading home."

Home. Wow, how easily I said that. I'd been in Destiny Falls for a month, but it felt like this was the home of my heart. It seemed like the place had waited for me and had welcomed me with open arms. The people here were related to me, but what made them family was far deeper than a blood connection. It seemed like I was the missing part of their puzzle, that I was an important part of the whole. I felt happy here.

"Are you okay, Hayden?" Han asked.

"Oh, sorry. Just lost in thought for a moment. It's really nice to see you, Han."

He gifted me with one of his gorgeous smiles. "Want some company on your walk home?"

"That would be lovely," I said. But what I meant was, "Ohhh, definitely yes!"

I started to walk, but was so smitten by his

smile, his nearness, and the idea that he might be my mystery man, that I nearly walked into a tree. He grabbed my arm just in time to save me. My hero.

"You okay there, Bambi?" he chuckled.

"Ha ha, my comical hero."

"Hero, eh? I like that." He put his arm around my shoulder and gave it a quick squeeze, then fell into step next to me as we walked together.

"So, Vessie's Hideaway Café? Have you ever seen so much pink in your life?" he asked.

"Maybe at the flamingo exhibit at the zoo," I said. "But I loved it, you know? Somehow it all works. And it seems to suit her personality."

"I agree. She's a sweetheart, so pink is appropriate. And she makes great coffee. What's on your agenda for the rest of the day?"

"I have an article I need to finish and I need to touch base with my business partner. Then family dinner tonight."

"Will that be fun?" he asked.

"Yes, it really will be! I never had a big family before. It's a touch overwhelming sometimes, but mostly, yeah, fun. Tomorrow will be special, though. I'm going to Sapphire's house for a girls' night with my two sisters."

"Nice to have sisters?" he asked.

"Oh, so nice! I never knew that I had a hole in my life until they filled it. There's just something different about a relationship when it carries that label."

I thought about it for a few minutes, trying to figure out how to explain my feelings. It was comforting that Han just walked quietly beside me as if he knew I was sorting it out and waiting patiently for me to finish my thought.

"Our relationship is new, but it's already powerful. It's like, you know, the connection will be there for the rest of your life, no matter what. It's a safe space where you can be yourself. Where you'll be accepted even when you aren't at your best. It makes you want to cherish the specialness of it. It will build into a strong, unbreakable bond. I feel it."

"That sounds about right. I have two younger sisters, you know?" Han said. "I know exactly what you mean. They're mine, for good times and bad, happy and sad. We can be serious or we can be goofy, but we always get each other. We have each other's backs. It's a profound connection that's bundled up in a tender exterior. Makes you want to shelter it from the world and keep it protected."

I smiled at Han. There was clearly so much more to him than his amazing smile and his incredibly sexy James Bond swagger.

5

Returning from my day in town, I found a note tacked to my bedroom door. On crisp white paper it said:

Tonight's dinner will take place in the garden.
The theme will be Family Game Night.
Please wear casual attire.

"Well, would you look at this?" I said to Latifa.

"How am I supposed to look, Sugar Cookie, when you're holding the paper waaay up there above my little head?"

"It's an invitation to family game night tonight." I held the paper out toward her. "That seems out of character for the Caldwell bunch. Casual attire? Since when? What games will they be playing, do you suppose?"

"Honey, there will be no lawn darts or water balloon toss, I guarantee it. So, don't you dare pull out shorts and a tank top."

She jumped down off the bed and made her way to the closet. A moment later she poked her head around the corner. *"Hellooo, Missy. Are you coming? It's fashion time."*

I joined Latifa in the closet, where she always enjoyed selecting my outfits. I could tell she'd been taking a break from the movie channel to watch *Project Runway* again, since she kept trying to overdo it, adding scarves and accessories and trying to pull together unusual items. I finally got her focused, so she was pacing the closet, thinking aloud.

"Sporty, not sloppy. Basic, not boring. Chic and classy, but casual. Hmmmm. Think, girl."

"I am thinking," I said.

"I'm not talking to you, dear."

I knew she was talking to herself and not me, but I couldn't resist. I pulled a floral-patterned T-shirt from the rack and waved it in front of her for inspection.

"Oh, goodness, no," she said. *"Fun, not frumpy, Mrs. Doubtfire. Tsk. What do you have in nautical colors? Stripes, perhaps?"*

She stretched out her neck and tried to nudge through my hanging clothes, but she was a little too short. I could tell this was going to take forever. I had an idea and went out to the bedroom and brought back the bench from the end of my bed.

"Well done! Now you're using that noggin' of yours," she said, jumping up onto the bench.

Now that she had a close-up look at my wardrobe, she made noises that sounded suspiciously like groans of despair.

"How am I to create the best possible outfit restricted by these selections?"

Yep. She'd been watching *Project Runway*

again. She ordered me around and had me try on various options that caught her eye. I was slightly annoyed, but I had to admit she had a good eye, so I held back on any snarkiness.

Soon, I was attired in a perfectly suitable outfit, according to Latifa. Sleeveless striped top with a sunny yellow summer jacket. She paired this with crisp white skinny jeans and flats. Her first choice was a pair of linen pants, but she suspected that I'd look wrinkled within an hour. I would. How do women wear linen pants and *not* look wrinkled?

We spent the next half hour sorting jewelry and accessories. So much for not taking forever.

"I must admit, this look is perfect," I said, putting on earrings for the final touch.

Latifa took a bow. *"Thank you, thank you. My work here is done."* With that, she proudly lifted her tail in the air and sauntered off to her alcove for a nap.

Latifa was cozied up asleep, which allowed me to catch up on my work and touch base with Luna.

I had decided not to tell Latifa or Axel about the odd conversation with Nakita, the ferry captain, or that I was planning to meet up with her. I knew it wasn't wise to slip away for that, but she had said not to tell anyone with that dire life or death warning. Plus, Vessie seemed to know her well, and she *was* the town's ferry captain. I decided it would be fine.

Before I knew it, the afternoon had slipped away, and it was time for dinner with the family.

I wasn't sure what to expect for a Caldwell Family Game Night. I knew it wouldn't be horse-shoes and a hot dog roast for this formal group, but I suspected something boring like cards, Bridge maybe. However, the backyard layout delighted my senses in a refreshing and unexpected way.

I was reminded of that scene in *Alice in Wonderland* where they play croquet with the Queen of Hearts, and then go to the Mad Hatter's tea party. The theme was hysterically appropriate, given the falling through the mirror thing. I would think they had to see the connection.

I stepped out of the door of the house through an archway made up of enormous-sized playing cards that were arranged to look like flowers.

The grassy section of the lawn was laid out with a croquet set. Not the ordinary backyard set. The mallets looked like upside-down pink flamin-goes and the wire arches were made of folded playing cards. The balls were painted to resemble hedgehogs, just like in the original scene.

Off to the side, a white party tent was set up with tables for dinner. The color scheme was a burst of playful pastels: blues, pinks, and greens. Chairs were adorned with large green bows, and the tables were covered in layered tablecloths:

green, angled over the top of sunny yellow. Each place setting contained a fanciful, patterned plate and an oversized teacup and saucer, many in polka dots and swirly patterns.

The tent was lined with tiny fairy lights and garlands hung with decorations: white rabbits, clock faces, and smiling Cheshire cats.

Once I absorbed the imaginative setting, I scanned the yard to see who was there. I was happy to see the entire family, plus a few extras, so I set out to touch base with everyone. This family was new to me, yet I felt a connection with them. And since I'd been to several events in this yard, it was becoming more comfortable for me to be here. One of these days, and I hoped it was soon, I'd bring Nana and Gran to one of these events. Oh, my! They would have an absolute blast.

I spotted my half-sister Indigo. I felt a rush of warmth at the sight of her. I was still reeling from the news that I had two previously hidden sisters. They were so kind, and they embraced our relationship with joyful enthusiasm. They were a blessing. And even more, I enjoyed their company.

Indigo and her husband Omar were standing with another tall, Black man who looked so much like Omar I had to guess that they were related. Their little son, Ian, was sitting in the grass next to them, playing with a girl who I assumed was the man's daughter. I went over and joined their group.

"Hi, Hayden! Great to see you," Indigo called

as I walked up.

She immediately drew me into a big hug. Ian's tiny arms wrapped around my leg. It always brought me great joy when he did that. I had never been around that many kids in my life, so I never knew what to expect. He was a little charmer with his wide smile and his affectionate embraces.

"Hello, Hayden," said Omar. "I'd like you to meet my brother, Dante."

I shook hands with Omar's look-alike brother. Then Dante introduced me to his daughter, Tiana. She seemed to be a little older than Ian, who was nearly five. I crouched down to the kids' level and said hello to Tiana.

"Your braids are so pretty! The beads look like they match the party decorations."

"Thank you," she said, ducking her head shyly. But I could see she was wearing a big grin.

"What are you creating?" I asked the kids. "I used to braid flowers. It's fun, isn't it?"

For the next few minutes, they showed me their creations; they were braiding flower stems into long chains. I hoped that Grandmother wouldn't be upset about the kids pulling flowers out of her perfect garden. I said as much, and the other adults laughed.

"Oh, you'll see," said Indigo. "She's fine with the children being creative."

I stood up and visited with the adults for a bit. Soon, my other sister Sapphire joined us. There was more hugging, more warm sisterly feelings, and more laughter.

Sapphire was a delightful and surprising sister. She was kind and polite in an almost Southern-girl style, and she dressed the part in floral dresses and sun hats. Interestingly, she was a computer tech specialist, and she had a mind like a steel trap. Sadly, her last boyfriend had been a disaster, and I hoped she'd soon find someone who really appreciated her. She deserved that.

As we chatted, Grandmother approached the group. I was momentarily speechless to see her perfectly-styled ensemble decorated by two flower-chain necklaces. So, apparently, the kiddos were safe picking flowers.

I felt a rush of warmth toward her. Eleanor had always frightened me a bit, and it took her weeks to thaw. But now I was seeing the kind woman who hid behind the rigid exterior. And like many women, her grandchildren and great-grandchildren seemed to bring out her soft side—well, and her Persian cat, Chanel. It was lovely to see the caring woman that she hid from the world.

I heard a ruckus from the other side of the yard. I looked over to see Axel goofing around with our youngest sibling, Cobalt, a university student often home for weekend family events. They were laughing loudly about something. Our father, Leonard, and our grandfather, Phillip, were looking puzzled. Clearly, they didn't get the joke. That seemed to make the guys laugh until they snorted.

Typical for Cobalt, but unlike the often too-serious Axel. I learned that my brothers had a tight bond and a relaxed relationship. It was heartwarming to see how Cobalt brought out the youthfulness in Axel.

Since everyone had arrived, Grandmother asked us to break up into teams for the game. Croquet was fun in theory, but in reality, it was a super boring game. One used the mallet to tap the ball around the yard through wire arched wickets—or in this case playing cards—until someone tapped the stake at the end. I had no idea how you count points, but maybe the first person to the end stake won. I was just guessing.

I was having a blast taking in the party décor, watching the family interact, and pretending to enjoy the croquet. Little did I know that the best was yet to come.

Cleobella, my grandmother's all-round assistant, came out of the house pushing a large cart of food. Two caterers were behind her, pushing their own carts.

True to form, Cleobella was dressed for the occasion. In a party catalog, her attire would be labeled 'sexy Queen of Hearts costume.' Her short dress was black, white, and red. It had a laced-up bodice and a black tutu, which was covered with red, glittering hearts. Her legs were clad in over-the-knee black socks with bright red bows above the knees. Her shoes were shiny black platform pumps. Her hair was curled into a wild halo of ringlets, and she was wearing a jaunty black, sparkly top hat. As usual, I could see her super-long eyelashes from across the yard. She was an eccentric sight to behold. But, as usual, I seemed to be the only person who thought so.

The two caterers coming up behind her looked uncomfortable, but dutiful, dressed as white rabbits. They were wearing large clock necklaces that would make Flavor Flav proud.

The food continued the Alice in Wonderland theme. Bright pink and blue multi-tiered trays were filled with finger sandwiches. Platters held mini tarts and scones. There were beautifully arranged platters of fruits and vegetables. Whimsically decorated cupcakes finished up the offerings. Between the food carts and Cleobella, it was a feast for the eyes.

Axel came up behind me and whispered, "I suppose you're wondering why nobody seems to notice Cleobella's, umm, interesting look?"

"Interesting is the understatement of the year."

"Yeah. She's always a fashion icon. We expect it. Every year she dresses up as the Queen of Hearts for the croquet event. Each time, it's a bit different, but always fun to see. I think we're all used to seeing her just as she is. This family is surprisingly more accepting of people's unique traits than you might think."

"I'm coming to understand that," I said.

"Did you see Grandmother's flower necklaces?"

"I did!" The thought of it made me smile. "I'm sure the kids were delighted to see her wearing them. It warmed my heart."

Axel nodded. "Grandmother is like a loaf of sourdough bread. Hard and crusty on the outside, soft and warm on the inside. But with a touch of tart flavoring to keep you on your toes."

"Don't I know that," I said.

Since the food had arrived, we were—happily—done with the game part of the evening. I thought I'd had enough croquet to last me for a good, long while.

As we were walking toward the tables, I saw a bit of white and chocolate brown fur in the bushes. I slowly meandered over. As I got closer, I could make out two pairs of feline eyes scanning the yard. Sure enough, Latifa and Chanel had hidden behind a bush to spy on us.

"Why are you outside, Latifa?" I asked. "You're a house cat, not a wildcat."

"Cats are born wild, Cupcake," she replied with a sniff. *"It's in their DNA. Taking a walk on the wild side is almost required."*

"You girls just be careful," I said.

"Okay, Mom." I could almost see her rolling her eyes. *"And hey, nice job on the ball-chasing game. You're almost good enough to be an honorary cat."*

The two of them snickered, turned their backs on me, and crept off toward the open back door.

6

In preparation for my meeting with the ferry captain, I was at the library to do some serious research about the ferry and our island location. I stood with my hand on the door to the library, hesitant to open it. I paused and took a deep breath. What would I find when I opened this door?

The exterior of the building looked the same as always. Charming small-town library. A cheery yellow building with white pillars framing the front door. Neatly mowed lawn with an orderly circle of flowers around the base of the flagpole. Lace curtains framing white-gridded windows. On my previous visits, it had turned out to be an elaborate disguise.

I hoped I wouldn't be walking into a normal library. I opened the door just a few inches and peeked inside. My breath whooshed out in relief, and I swung the door open and stepped inside.

True to form for Destiny Falls' enchanted library, wonders greeted me in the expansive foyer. Even though it was morning outside, it was nighttime here. The ceiling, very high above me, wasn't a ceiling at all. It was a night sky. Wider, deeper, and more intense than any planetarium could hope to be. It looked real. And it probably was.

The deep blue above me was awash with stars, like what I would see from a mountaintop. On one side I could pick out the Big Dipper and on the other, Orion's belt. Off in the distance, the northern lights were flowing and dancing in brilliant shades of green, purple, and blue.

The white-curtained windows that I saw from outside did not exist in here. Instead, clerestory windows surrounded the uppermost area, reaching almost to the, um, night sky. Through the windows, I could see the full moon in the distance.

Signs placed around the lobby helped visitors locate various constellations and other celestial wonders in the night sky above us. A display table provided binoculars for patron use, and several telescopes were available for even closer viewing of the celestial bodies.

A bookshelf lined the back wall with an array of books on astronomical topics, along with videos and audiobooks. There was an area with reclining chairs for those who had tired of craning their necks. Two little kids were in the children's corner, placing flannel stars, planets, comets, and satellites on a large flannel board. Talk about an immersive learning opportunity!

I spent an awestruck hour soaking in this experience, then reluctantly left to get to the real reason I was here—a visit to the historical books room to see if I could learn anything about the ferry before my appointment tomorrow.

I was also looking forward to spending

some time with my favorite librarian and historian, Edna. She was a wonder! She could magically produce any book that a patron requested, plus more books that they didn't even know they needed. The library appeared to work alongside Edna to meet the needs of the community. She said that only once did it keep a secret from her, though I expect it either hid more secrets than she knew, or she hid secrets from me.

"Hayden! Wonderful to see you," Edna called out in her whispery librarian voice.

The acoustics in the building were remarkable. No matter how many people were inside, and no matter how loudly I spoke, all I'd ever hear was the soft blend of quiet murmurs. The environment encompassed everything that was best in the world. The smell of old books and wood polish was intoxicating. The soft lighting gave everything a golden glow that was unique to a library filled with everything from romance paperbacks to ancient, leather-bound tomes. And books, glorious books, surrounded me, capturing nearly every inch of space.

A gorgeous, wide staircase connected the three stories of books. Usually, when I looked up, I saw a massive chandelier at the top. Today, though, in keeping with the theme, it was an enormous model of the solar system. Each planet was lit from within, and all of them were very slowly making their way around the brilliant sun.

I assumed that wires must connect them, but I couldn't see any. Then again, here in this magical building, anything was possible.

Edna approached silently on her high-top sneakered feet and gave me a quick hug. It seemed like everyone I'd met in Destiny Falls was warm, friendly, and prone to hugging. It was quite nice.

"How are you, Edna?" I asked.

"Happy, as always. How about you? Settling into the Destiny Falls lifestyle? It's been about a month, hasn't it?"

"It has. It's been a bit of a roller-coaster, but things are smoothing out."

"I'm glad! That bit about Gwendolyn was horrifying." She shuddered. "How's your knee?"

"Pretty much back to normal," I said. "I'm back to jogging and hiking, thankfully. I jogged into town with Axel yesterday. We visited Poppy's new extravaganza and Vessie's café. Both are wonderful! Have you been?"

"Oh, Vessie's is my normal coffee stop on my way to work. She makes the best muffins and lattes. I haven't been to Poppy's store, but I hear it's amazing. It got me thinking I should get some hiking supplies and check out the park. It's on my to-do list now."

I recalled that Poppy had said that the town's plan was to get people hiking and camping. Seemed it was working.

"Oh! You really should," I told her. "Twin Falls Park is a gorgeous place, and so peaceful. I think you'd love it."

We talked a bit more about the park and trails. I enjoyed chatting with Edna. She was enthusiastic about everything, and when I talked, she really listened. She was one of those people who made everyone feel important by looking deep into their eyes, nodding, and um-hmming at exactly the right moments.

"Would I be able to get into the historic book room? I'd like to do some research."

"Of course!" Edna pulled out her key ring, and I followed her up the stairs.

The historic book room was at the end of a secluded hallway. A select few people could enter it. Edna, of course, as the librarian and historian. And apparently, me. It appeared being a Caldwell had its privileges.

The small room had bookshelves on all four walls. The center was a reading and working space. The last few times I had been here, the area in the center had a set of leather furniture. The focal point was an amazing coffee table that was made up of a huge fish aquarium with a glass top suspended above it on brass legs. Today it was totally different.

The center of the room continued the space theme from downstairs. The entire area had a dome above it that carried the night sky theme, but this one was painted, not a live night sky. Hanging from the very center was a light fixture made of thousands of tiny blue and white star-shaped bulbs. The tables were silver, the chairs were white leather, and the floor was white granite. The furniture was lit from beneath with a blue glow. It felt very sci-fi.

On my last trip here, I had tried to find out more about the ferry. But I discovered little of interest. The books, just like the people here, seemed elusive and stingy with details. I scrolled through my pictures, looking for the pages I had saved on my phone. This seemed the most helpful, yet confusing section:

. . . The Destiny Falls ferry does not have a regular schedule as its daily routes change depending on the passengers. The ferry travels only to a few select ports, and some passengers attempting to reach locations in the Outside often find themselves getting off exactly where they first got on . . .

Searching for ferry information had led to a dead-end, so I thought a fresh approach might yield more information. I asked Edna where I could find books on the geography of the area, specifically, the islands surrounding us. She showed me the various options and left me to my research.

On her way out, she turned back to me. "It's great to see you, Hayden. Take your time in here. Ring the bell if you need any help. Always remember to lock up when you leave the room."

She said that every time she left me here. I

wondered why a door lock was even necessary. If the library were enchanted, wouldn't it have a way to protect all these historic and valuable books? Something far more powerful than a mere door lock?

I scanned the shelves, pulled out a stack of choices, and carried them over to the table. As always, at some point during my book search, Edna —I assumed!—had come back in and left a tray of tea and cookies on the table, along with a welcome note. It always made me feel like I belonged here. I poured a cup of tea, helped myself to the cookies, and settled in to sift through my pile of books.

An hour later, I huffed in frustration. Once again, the information I found was limited. Maps showed Destiny Falls in detail, but the surrounding areas were blurred out or simply not shown at all. I stood up and stretched, looking around the room. I spotted an enormous globe that I hadn't seen before. Or more accurately, that hadn't been there before. It was lit from within, like the planets had been, and was sitting on a pedestal with a softly glowing blue base.

I twirled the globe to find Destiny Falls. As of now, I had no idea where we were in the world, though hints pointed to the United States.

Since the ferry was located on Caldwell Harbor and I could see mountains off in the distance, I scanned all the inlets, gulfs, and bays along the coasts. I ran my finger along the surface and traced the coastline. I came to an unusual notch on the west coast. I peered closely. It was too small to see clearly, so I took a photo with my phone and enlarged it. The notch did not appear in my photo. That had to be the work of the DF Satellite, which filtered transmissions and only allowed approved texts, e-mails, and calls. Approved by whom I had no idea.

A glimmer of reflected light caught my eye, and I found a magnifying glass on a shelf to my right. It appeared that the library was on my side this morning. I stepped away to grab the magnifying glass.

The globe had rotated a bit when I moved away from it, so I searched again for the coastline with the notch. I found it. In an entirely different place than where it had been a minute ago. I shut my eyes and spun the globe. And found the inlet in the area facing me. Twice more. No matter how I twirled the globe, the inlet was facing me. Apparently, I was invited to explore the group of islands, but where we were located on the globe was still top secret . . . or not applicable. I quickly dismissed that thought.

I used the magnifying glass to inspect the area. There had to be a cluster of more than a hundred islands in this inlet. Only the largest islands had names shown. I knew our town name was Destiny Falls, and the ferry docked at Caldwell Harbor, but I didn't know the name of the island, as I'd never heard our location called anything other than Destiny Falls.

Just then, Edna walked into the room to check on me. Her eyes popped open wide and her jaw dropped. "Oh, my!" she whispered. "You've been granted a view of the globe!"

"And even a magnifying glass!" I held it up.

"Hayden, you are one of the privileged few. The library rarely brings the globe out."

I looked up toward the ceiling. "I feel honored. Thank you, library," I said.

Edna giggled. "I know exactly how you feel."

I could feel the color creeping up my face. I felt silly, but the library did feel like a real being at times.

"I'm trying to find Destiny Falls on here, but there are so many islands and the words are tiny. Do you know where we are on here? And is the actual island called Destiny Falls?"

"Yes, Destiny Falls is the name of the island and the community."

Oh, my God! A straightforward answer for once! I was shocked, but tried not to show it. Perhaps since the globe had appeared to me, Edna felt permitted to share more information. She walked over to the globe, leaned down, and pointed. "Here we are," she said.

I brought up the magnifying glass and looked at the island. Sure enough, it was labeled Destiny Falls. I could see what appeared to be Caldwell Harbor and the area where the ferry was located.

The Destiny Falls island was shaped like a crescent. Just across from it was another island of similar size and shape, but in reverse. It looked like it fit the shoreline of Destiny Falls as precisely as a puzzle piece. It was labeled Gladstone. The word the ferry captain had uttered in the same sentence as *danger*.

7

I left the library and was analyzing the experience in my head. When I had found Gladstone on the globe and asked Edna about it, she had said she knew little about it and changed the subject. I found that extremely odd, considering that she was the town historian and appeared to know everything about the community. The mysteries around here sometimes gave me a headache. I had to poke, prod, and persist to gain any bit of information about the town and its people. That was okay. I was a journalist by trade and, according to some people, a bit of a busybody, so I would just continue my informal investigation. Beginning with my meeting with the captain tomorrow.

I thought I would walk around town before heading home. I strolled over to the bench across from the ferry terminal and sat down. I thought I'd sit for a while, enjoy the view, and observe the ferry landing.

The ferry wasn't there, but people were gathering in the area, waiting for the next sailing. I saw several families and groups assembled and a few cars in line. I could see the things that walk-on passengers carried, and some things that were inside the cars in line. Most people had beach blankets, blow-up floats, picnic baskets, and other supplies that signaled a fun day at the beach. Luckily for them, it seemed it was always sunny and warm here, so it was easy to plan for this kind of outing.

Oddly, there was one group of people with SUVs loaded up with skis, snowshoes, parkas, and other winter sports paraphernalia. That was strange, as I'd only ever seen a small ferry here, one that carried a hundred cars at the most. I didn't think the route would be long enough to get to a wintery stop. Could mountains be that high that one could go from a warm beach to skiing on the same island? That was unlikely. I'd heard of places where skiing is three or four hours from the beach, but I didn't think that these islands were big enough for that kind of situation.

Scanning the line of cars, and the group of people waiting for the ferry, I noticed more odd differences. Some people looked like they were going to work for the day, wearing business attire and carrying just a purse and a briefcase. Others had large rolling suitcases or carts piled with supplies. A family was saying goodbye to a young man dressed in a military-style uniform, and the mother was hugging him and crying. I wondered if this ferry went to a military port. An airport was highly unlikely in a small chain of islands. One would think he'd go inland if he were traveling overseas. That is, if Destiny Falls let him out. It made me wonder if everyone here were as trapped as my father and I were.

People appeared to be getting tickets at a small office on the dock. However, I noticed that the skiers from the SUVs went around to the back of the building and returned holding their tickets. Hmm. Was there a different ticket booth for the mountain stop? Several of the skiers saw me sitting across the road and yelled hello. They started to walk my way. As they got closer to me, they stopped and called out, "Oh, sorry! Thought you were someone else." Then they turned and headed back to their cars. It was strange that this kept happening. It seemed to occur only here at the ferry terminal.

I saw the ferryboat coming in and the dock crew preparing for its arrival. People walked back to their cars and walk-on passengers gathered near the dock. This ferry was twice as large as the one I had seen before. Did it change size and shape like the library and Caldwell Crest? Or was it an absolutely normal fact of the harbor having more than one ferry?

It was time for me to get back home since I had work to catch up on. Continuing to help my business partner run our magazine remotely was taking some adjustment. It seemed to work fine as long as I kept to my schedule. Which meant today was a writing day and I had an article to finish. I needed to get it done since tonight was the girls' night I had planned with my sisters. I had my eye on the ice cream stand and thought I'd grab a cone and enjoy it on my walk home. One single scoop of fruit sorbet would be sensible.

I walked across the street and up to the window. The list of available choices was astounding. There were a dozen flavors I wanted to try. The names alone demanded that I be adventurous. I ended up ordering a scoop of Razzle Dazzle Raspberry topped with a scoop of Chunky Chocolate Caramel.

I was pulling a few napkins from the dispenser when the ticket office loudspeaker crackled to life. I expected to hear a boarding announcement. Instead, I heard something unexpected. "We regret to inform you that all of today's sailings have been cancelled. Please exit the terminal area. Tickets may be exchanged or refunded online or by calling the ferry office." The voice repeated the message with more urgency, "Please exit the terminal area immediately."

At that moment, Sheriff Jaxson Redford's car pulled up to the terminal with lights flashing. A second patrol car pulled up alongside his. As much as I wanted to know what was happening, I knew it was prudent to stay put and out of the way.

I looked up to see Vessie coming out of her café. She walked across the street and stood next to me.

"What's happening?" she asked me.

"I have no idea. An announcement was made cancelling the rest of the day's trips. They asked everyone to leave the boarding area."

An ambulance pulled up to the curb and I saw Jaxson directing traffic to move cars out of the way to allow the ambulance room to pull up close to the disembarking ramp. The ferry staff was preventing cars and people from getting off the boat, and I recognized the two huge men in mechanic's uniforms whom I had seen in the café.

The only people disembarking appeared to be a group of crew members. I could see the two mechanics plus Kerbie's short, bright, red head in the group. Several of the workers were carrying something large between them.

"What is that they're carrying?" I asked Vessie.

We heard a collective gasp from the people around us and someone said, "Oh, my God! They have someone on a stretcher!"

The crew walked directly to the ambulance and the medical workers loaded the stretcher into the vehicle. Once they had loaded the patient, the ambulance pulled away. The crew made another announcement, directing the lingering people to leave the area.

Vessie and I walked across the street and sat on the bench in front of her café.

Once the ambulance left and they cleared the immediate area, we saw Jaxson walking across the street toward us. His hat was in his hand, and he was wiping the back of his sleeve across his brow. He looked intense. When he had this look on his face, it was like he was a different person from the lighthearted friend of my brother. He was in Sheriff Redford mode.

"Hayden. Vessie." He nodded at us. That was uncharacteristically terse for him. "Can I get your largest coffee to go? It's going to be a very long day."

"Sure, Jax," said Vessie. "What happened over there? It looks like someone was injured?"

"Actually, a death onboard. They found the body during the voyage. Severe head injuries. We're not clear if the attack occurred during the voyage or before sailing."

"Was it a passenger?" I asked.

"No," he said. "It was Nakita Morozova. The ferry captain."

My ice cream cone slipped out of my hand, the pink and brown colors squashing together in an unnoticed heap on the pavement.

8

Latifa was hiding under the bed. All I could see was the tip of her nose and her big round eyes. She was the best listener, unless she was being overly dramatic.

"I am not being dramatic, Sister. This stuff is real," she huffed, as she crawled out from under the bed and sat at my feet.

I seriously needed to learn how to veil my thoughts from her. That would be hard to do since I had no idea how this telepathy communication worked. Most of the time I was glad I could talk to my cat, but there were times when I would have liked to filter her out.

"Filter me out! Hayden, you crush me." Her little shoulders drooped, and she looked up at me in the same sweet, vulnerable pose that the cat in the Shrek movies uses to manipulate people. No wonder she had mastered the look. It worked.

"I'm sorry, Latifa. You know I love you," I said.

"Forgiven." The fake vulnerable pose was gone in a snap. *"So, you were saying, you saw a dead body?"*

"Well, no. I didn't actually see the body. I saw a stretcher being loaded onto an ambulance. Jaxson told me that someone had died."

"Who? Who died? Why are you being so evasive?" She squinted her eyes at me.

At that moment, I realized that it was time to come clean and tell Latifa everything. Since no one else could communicate with her, it was safe to share my secrets with her. And I desperately needed someone to talk to. My heart was still racing from that moment I knew that the ferry captain has been murdered.

Talking through things with Latifa would also be helpful, as it would enable me to verbalize what I knew and help me sort things through. I could voice all my concerns and share my suspicions. Plus, besides her being a good sounding board, Latifa would often provide some wonderful insights.

"There's a story behind all this," I said. "Let me start at the beginning."

"The beginning of what? The dead body? Should I be taking notes?" She batted at a pencil she spotted on the floor. *"But sadly, no opposable thumbs,"* she sighed.

"Do you want me to tell you?" I scowled at her.

"Sorry . . . Captain Serious." She gave a mock salute with her furry paw. *"Please, continue."*

"Yesterday Axel and I jogged into town, and he took me to Vessie's Hideaway Café."

"The pink palace." She nodded as if she knew the place.

"How do you know about Vessie's?" I asked.

"Vessie's cat, Marshmallow, is a friend of Chanel's. I met her the other day, and she was talking about the café. That's what she calls it, the pink palace."

"Latifa! It sounds like you're living a clandestine life right behind my back!"

"Not hiding anything, Chica. It just never came up. So, you were at Vessie's?"

"Right. I was waiting for my tea and oatmeal," I started.

"Goodness, girl. Eat something different once in a while."

I stopped talking and just stared at my cat.

"Oops, my bad." She sat up and crossed her paws, tilted her head, and gave me an 'I'm listening' pose.

"While I was waiting for my breakfast, there were two people in line. The helmsman. He's the guy that drives the boat. And the ferry captain, Nakita. She followed me down the hall and was acting quite suspicious. She told me a secret."

"Oooo. A secret?"

"Right. She said that she had something for me. And that I should go to the ferry terminal to learn more. But here's the scary part. She said not to tell anyone about this. She said it was life or death! She warned me that—for the safety of my family—I should trust no one."

"Hoo-leee cow," Latifa gasped.

"It was unnerving. I've been going over it in my mind since it happened. I didn't want to say anything to anyone because of her warning. But I know I can tell you."

She nodded. *"Um-hmm."*

"The captain also said something about 'Gladstone' and danger, but she was whispering and shushing me, so I couldn't hear everything she was saying. Gladstone is the name of the island that Olivia and Edna would not discuss with me."

"Geeze. That's bizarre. But what does she have to do with the dead body?" Latifa asked.

"It was the captain! She was the dead body! I talked to her. I planned to meet her. And then I saw her dead body!"

Latifa's mouth opened in a gasp, and she zipped under the bed again. In a minute, she peeked out.

"Ohhh. So, now she's dead. And you don't have the thing. And you don't know the secret."

"Yes, exactly." Telling her all this had elevated my stress levels again. I sat on the floor and put my head in my hands.

We were both silent for several long minutes.

"And the dead person told you not to tell anyone. Because it was 'life or death.' But now she's the dead one."

"Latifa! Please stop saying 'dead.'"

"Sorry," she said. Then, in the tiniest little whisper, *"Dead."*

Latifa was spooked after our conversation,

so she retreated to her alcove for a nap. I was back to pacing the room, thinking through everything that had happened. *What should I do now?* It seemed that the secret was even more dangerous than I had first thought. The woman's threats were all too real. What was the thing that she was going to give me? What were the secrets that she was going to tell me?

My thoughts were in a jumble, and I had a hard time processing them in any reasonable manner. I stopped walking and gaped at a door. An entirely new door that had appeared next to my bookcase.

Normally, there were two doors near my bookcase. One to the en-suite bathroom, and one to the closet. Today, there was a third door.

There was a time in my life, okay, just a month ago, when a mysterious door just appearing in my bedroom would be cause for concern. Now, it meant something good. Well, almost for sure it would be something good. I opened it to see what surprise awaited me.

"Oh, my . . ." I exhaled the words and stepped into the room.

What I saw nearly took my breath away. It appeared that the house knew I was stressed and terrified. It had created a soothing recovery room, meant for yoga and meditation. The far wall was made entirely of windows. Where the water was usually a hundred or more feet away from the home, far past the gardens, here the water came right up to the windows. It almost felt like I was on a dock or a boat. As I stepped closer, I realized these weren't windows. They were sliding glass doors. I felt drawn to step outside and dip my feet in the glistening water, which I would definitely do later.

The room was mostly empty, with several large yoga mats in swirling pale purple and green. In one corner was a pile of lounging pillows surrounded by potted plants and palm trees. In the other corner, there was a tall, brass water feature with trickles of water flowing down a tower of rocks.

The walls of the room were painted a pale blue, with one wall covered in bamboo. A large teardrop mirror hung on the wall from a braided rope.

I was taking in the room's beauty when a white shape appeared in the teardrop mirror. I turned toward it, but it was gone. It must have been a reflection. A moment later, there was another flicker of white, but as quickly as it appeared, it was gone again.

As I walked over to look closely at the brass water feature, I again caught a flicker of white in the mirror, so I walked over to stand in front of it. Oh, my gosh! I was looking into my Nana and Granana's home in Seattle!

I wondered if Caldwell Crest understood my anxiety and felt that a glimpse of my family home would bring me some sense of calm, which would allow me to make a reasonable plan.

I was looking in the mirror at their living room when suddenly, there it was again—the white blur!

I realized that the white blur was the top of Gran's white-haired head! She was in the living room. There it was again! Up and down. Yes, it was my great-grandmother! She was doing her step aerobics!

I got closer to the mirror. I waved my arms and called out to her. But of course, her back was to me, so she couldn't see me. True to the history of the mirrors, she couldn't hear me either.

Rooted to the spot, I watched helplessly as she continued bouncing up and down on her step, with no idea that I was watching her. Then, she reached her hands up into the air, her fingers wiggling. She was doing her 'stretching' as she called it.

Workout complete, she picked up her folding step and her towel and walked out of the room. I sagged in disappointment. I missed her and my nana so much. This had been a very long and intense day, at the end of a very long and intense month. It was especially difficult to handle all of this without their calming presence.

I hoped that the vision in the mirror was a good sign. If the house felt I could view them, perhaps the next step was actual communication. Then, I hoped, would come a day when I could bring them here for a visit. I held onto that warm feeling and sank down on one of the yoga mats to see if I could clear my head and make a plan.

9

I was so grateful to the house for my new yoga room. After an hour in that remarkably peaceful place, I was more clear-headed. Followed up by a shower and a change of clothes, I felt renewed and ready for my first official girls' night with my sisters.

I'd really gotten to know my brother Axel over the past month, but I'd had little time to get to know Cobalt, Indigo, and Sapphire. Cobalt was still attending the university, so I knew that would happen in bits and pieces. Tonight's visit with my sisters would be our first real quality time together.

Spending tonight with them would also allow me to distance myself from the horror of the ferry captain's murder and the mystery of the secrets she had left unsaid. As hard as it is for me to keep secrets, I had absolutely zero intention of telling my sisters anything, since that warning of danger to my family would keep me quiet. I would set aside my worry and fears to focus on getting to know my sisters.

As I made my way down to the front door, I heard voices coming from the living room, so I peeked in. I was shocked to see a girls' night of a different kind.

My sneaky cat and her beautiful Persian partner-in-crime were batting at a feathered cat toy being held aloft by none other than Poppy of the Camping Extravaganza. My grandmother was sitting at a table playing chess with Cleobella. Several bottles of wine and platters of appetizers were spread on the two coffee tables. Rod Stewart's distinctive raspy voice filled the room. Grandmother having *fun?* What a bewildering notion! Who knew it was possible?

The sisters were dressed for the event in colorful footed pajamas. I had no idea that they made those in adult sizes. Poppy was in head-to-toe pink, covered with red and white hearts. Cleobella wore bright white, splattered with rainbow-colored polka dots. Their hair was twisted and braided into tall, whimsical Whoville updos. Of course, they were both in full stage makeup, spider-like eyelashes, with bold, shiny lips included.

What was uniquely delightful was seeing my rigid, formal grandmother in glamourous, dark blue silk pajamas, edged in crisp white piping. On her feet were a pair of feathered, high-heeled slippers, and I could have sworn I saw a tattooed rose on her ankle. That woman was almost more mysterious than this house.

I don't know how long I'd been standing in the doorway staring, but I suddenly realized that all five heads were turned in my direction. I said hello and they all waved. Well, the people waved. The cats just stared at me.

"I'm off to Sapphire's house. Have a great evening," I said.

"Buh bye, toots!" Latifa said.

Axel had given me keys to one of the family cars, with the code and instructions for garage number six. There were eight stalls now since the house added a place for every car brought into the family. I was told this was a three-car garage many years ago. When I opened the garage door, I was overjoyed to see a smart, red Fiat Spider convertible. It wasn't a long drive to Sapphire's house, but it would be a fun one!

The drive was exhilarating. And I easily wound my way through town. Sapphire's home was a total surprise—not that I'd had many of those this past month. With her sweet, Southern-girl aura, I expected a farm-style house with a wraparound deck housing a porch swing. Instead, here she flew her tech wizard flag. Her home was a big, white, modern-looking square, with an angular design that must have been created by a talented architect, because it was more art than a house. It had large windows that allowed the best views of the waterfront of Caldwell Harbor. I pulled into the driveway just as a flurry of flowered sundresses came bursting out of the front door. My sisters. They looked just as excited to see me as I was to see them. Their warm smiles instantly made me feel welcome.

"Hayden, hello!" Sapphire called. I walked up the front steps and she welcomed me with hugs and affectionate greetings.

"I've been so looking forward to this," said Indigo. "Girls' night rocks!"

Indigo took me by the arm and guided me inside. I loved the modern, artsy feel of the home. With sleek lines and open spaces, it was decorated in white, gray, and chrome, but with vivid splashes of modern art and accents in bold colors. Colorful pillows filled up the soft, white sofa, which centered the living space in a giant horseshoe. Plenty of houseplants and a wall filled with family photos brought a homey warmth to the décor.

With all the fancy, glistening white, I was charmed to see two steaming pizza boxes on the kitchen counter. Indigo asked if I liked margaritas —I do!—and she went into the kitchen and began preparing a pitcher.

Within minutes, I was swept up into their warm hospitality. In truth, it was so much more than that. It was that feeling of sisterhood that I had talked to Han about. A connection that was deeper than friendship, but lighter too. I felt free to be me and to accept them for who they were.

The conversation was easy, the topics fun, and as free-flowing as the margaritas. As the pizza disappeared and the pitcher emptied, the chatter became more open and honest. The conversation turned to family. They told stories about Axel and

Cobalt that I was sure the guys would have found too embarrassing to share. But it just highlighted the light, sometimes goofy, relationship between the guys, which always brought me so much joy to witness.

"So, tell me about Jade," I said. Jade was their mother, but apparently, she never grasped the idea of motherhood. Our father raised the girls. It didn't seem like they had a very good relationship with her, but even so, she was always around at family events, which was a little odd.

Sapphire blew out a big breath. "Not sure what's to tell. She had three kids, then divorced our dad. They never got along." She shrugged. "I suspect it was immaculate conception." She and Indigo doubled over with laughter at that comment.

"That's not even what that means!" Indigo said through her sputters. "You mean they probably never had sex!"

"Ewww! Stop!" Sapphire fell backwards on the sofa and covered her face with her hands. I could still hear her chortling.

When they finally settled down and began sipping their margaritas again—not that they needed any more—they continued talking about Jade and our father.

"Grandmother said Dad only got married to have kids. He wanted siblings for Axel. Once that was done, ptttt." Sapphire tried to snap her fingers, but didn't quite succeed.

"She never said that," corrected Indigo.

"Well, she *implied* it," said Sapphire, using finger quotes around the word implied. "She also *implied*" —again with finger quotes— "that Dad never got over the heartbreak of his first love, so he never gave Jade a chance. It was doomed from the start. She *impliiied*,"—finger quotes around the elongated word—"that's also why he never remarried. Truuuue love, forever lost."

"You're not even using the *finger quotes* properly," said Indigo, using finger quotes around the words *finger quotes*.

They both started chortling again, then suddenly Indigo straightened up in her seat and looked shocked into being serious.

"Oh, my God." She looked at me with wide eyes and covered her mouth with both hands. Then she shook her head. "I'm so sorry, Hayden! Dad's first love was your mother! Emily was your mother! Sapphire, did you hear me? Emily was Hayden's mother! So, we shouldn't be talking about this."

"Oooh no. I'm sooo sorry," said Sapphire, trying hard to be sober, but slurring her words.

"No, guys, it's okay," I said. "Really. It's more than okay. My nana and gran never talked about my mother. I mean, like never. This is the first time anyone has ever talked about her. Please. Keep talking. I never knew any of this. What else do you know?"

Indigo seemed to gain a bit of soberness. "Let's switch to coffee, then we can make more sense."

Indigo and Sapphire bungled around the kitchen for a bit, laughing and bumping into each other as they made a pot of coffee. Watching them together created a tightness in my chest and a lump formed in my throat. I blinked back my tears and took a deep breath. Sisters were better than I could have imagined.

We took our coffee outside and sat in the comfortable lounge chairs. We quietly sipped our drinks. The seating area on the deck had a picture-perfect view of the harbor and the starry night sky. It was peaceful here.

After a while, I broke the silence. "So, what do you know about my mother?" I asked.

"Well, no one ever sat down and talked about her," said Indigo. "It's more the bits and pieces we picked up over time. I know she was beautiful and that she sang like an angel. Dad let that slip once when I was about seven and sang in the school play."

"I know he could never understand why she left the baby. That would be little baby you, Hayden!" said Sapphire, still a bit tipsy and surprised at the connection. "He said she was made to be a mother, and she took to it from the moment she knew she was pregnant with Axel. I heard him telling Grandmother that once when he complained that Jade had no mothering instincts at all."

Indigo chimed in. "I heard that she was devoted to Axel and didn't put him down for the first three months of his life. She even slept with him right beside her. And if anyone tried to tell her that it was extreme, she shut them down like an angry mother lion."

Sapphire nodded. "And apparently, she was a kind, patient mother. The exact opposite of Jade. One time I heard Jade and Dad fighting. She was yelling and blamed his lack of love for her on Emily and said she refused to be compared to an invisible saint. Those were her exact words. An invisible saint."

"Wow," I said. "If she was such a devoted mother, how could she leave her newborn baby and never look back?"

Indigo shook her head. "Dad said it made no sense that she'd leave, but he'd never elaborate. He shut down any questions we had. He said it was ancient history and not to be dug up."

After all those revelations, we chatted quietly about less intense topics until we all started to yawn. We cleaned up our dishes and I thanked them profusely for such a wonderful evening.

"No thanks necessary, sweetheart," said Indigo "That's what sisters are for."

10

The Witch

High at the top of a mountain, overlooking Destiny Falls, was a cave. It was no ordinary cave. Well, it once was an ordinary cave, but that was many years ago. Now, it was home to an angry, exiled witch.

The witch was in a terrible mood. And because of that, hikers who made their way near would often hear the disturbing howl of a wild animal. Some thought it was a coyote, some swore it was a bizarre owl. The truth was that it was the witch's nightly cry. She had suffered through the second of her near successful attempts at escape. Twice in forty years! And both times, she'd been so close, yet failed because of the ineptitude of the minions she had chosen to aid her.

She had finally created the perfect potion, but those fools did not complete the steps necessary for it to work. Now, it would not perform as planned. It had become too weak. Within the potion was hidden a special jolt that would have broken her free of this dungeon-like cave.

In her despair following this failure, she had used up some unused potion to remodel part of her cave. She'd created a replica of the genie's bottle from her favorite show, *I Dream of Jeanie*. She had already grown tired of the ridiculous purple velvet, the gazillion fancy throw pillows, and the freakin' shiny sequins everywhere.

While she loved looking young and beautiful again, she'd grown bored with dressing in the harem outfit and braiding her long, now-blond hair. She'd take that low-maintenance, white hairdo any day. Yet she was saving up the leftover potion for something bigger. That meant she was stuck in her Jeanie world for a while longer. She was angry at herself for using some of the magic so frivolously.

It wasn't even her fault she was stuck here. It was all because of her two wretched sisters and her horribly cruel father. The anger that festered inside her was deep and powerful.

Now, at last, one of her sisters was being sloppy. And, in her blunder, she had left an opening. An opening that turned this angry witch positively giddy with possibilities. It was time to try something different.

11

The glow from last evening with my sisters remained with me and it carried me through my morning.

"Oh, Latifa! Having sisters is life-enhancing! My run felt shorter and lighter. The day seems sunnier. I even think my oatmeal was tastier."

"Oy with the poetry, already. I get it. You had fun at girls' night."

"It was more than just fun, Latifa. It was transcendent. Having sisters is life-changing."

"Speaking of life-changing, your grandmother's going to call you down to her office this morning."

"How do you know that?" I asked her.

She just stared at me, as if I should know that answer.

"Oh. Chanel."

Just then my phone pinged. A text message from Cleobella. This was momentous. It was the first time she'd ever texted me. It felt oddly exhilarating. As if a sign that I was now a real member of this family.

Your grandmother requests your presence in her office in one hour.

Thank you, Cleobella. I'll be there.

Of course you will.

One would think that might be offensive, but she was just being honest.

"Looks like you're right, I've been summoned. And if Grandmother beckons, you go. There isn't any other option."

"Well, I suppose if you were dead you wouldn't show up," said Latifa. *"But that would be the only excuse the grande dame would accept."* She giggled, then spoke with an English accent for some reason, *"Oh, sorry, Madam. Can't make it today, I'm dead."*

"Can you please shelve the death references? I'm still shell-shocked from the ferry captain's demise."

"Ah! I can't say dead, but I can say demise? Hmm. How about departed? Expired? Kaput?"

"None of those, please." I shuddered with the memory. "I have time to squeeze in a bit of yoga, and then, if you're a good cat, you can help me pick an outfit."

"You know you'd let me help, even if I wasn't a good cat. You can't manage to dress properly without me, Doll. And let's be honest, you're going to peek in the teardrop mirror again, aren't you? I've been watching you sneak in there."

"Can you blame me?" I said as I opened the door to my yoga room and walked directly over to the teardrop mirror. Ever since I saw Granana's little white head as she did her step aerobics, it had only been acting like a normal mirror. But I knew it couldn't be a one-time thing.

My body tensed up, and I gritted my teeth, ready for another disappointment. I looked in the mirror, ready to see my own reflection. I let out a little shriek of delight. I knew it would happen again!

I could see Nana and Gran in the kitchen. By the sheer number of leftovers on the counter, I knew they were making what Gran called her 'concoction.' That basically meant eggs with all the leftovers she could toss in, scrambled together and overcooked, as always. She liked to beat the eggs into submission until they were little bits of egg rice.

The two of them were so engaged and too far away to see me in the mirror, but I still felt elated just to see them. And now I felt hope. Sorry, Latifa; I'd be sneaking in here all the time now.

My heart felt even fuller, and my yoga seemed like a message of gratefulness out to the universe. I took a deep breath in and out, then heard another deep breath behind me. I turned around and saw Latifa and Chanel stretched out into somewhat yoga-ish poses.

"Good morning, Chanel," I said.

"*She says, good day to you, Miss Hayden,*" Latifa translated the meow.

The cats and I finished up our yoga session.

I was thankful no one was videotaping. And oh joy! I had two fashion critics helping me select a meeting-with-the-grandmother outfit. At least Chanel's comments were on point and helpful. Latifa was still on her *Project Runway* kick, which basically meant mixing odd colors and fabrics and trying to overload me with accessories, none of which I would wear this morning.

"Good morning, Grandmother." I gave her a quick hug. It felt like hugging a tree, but a tree with a slight smile on her face. My father was sitting across from the desk. I gave him a quick hug, too. I left off a name for him whenever we spoke. Father felt too stiff, but I barely knew him, so Dad was totally out of the question. It was just a touch awkward for me, but he didn't seem to notice. Or perhaps he was just allowing me time to adjust. We were slowly getting to know each other, and it was clear he was trying hard to build our connection. I appreciated that and felt my affection growing for this man, but something like that took time.

I'd always been told my father had abandoned us, left when I was just hours old, taking my toddler brother with him. We never knew why, and no one talked about it. We were unaware that he hadn't left by choice. Destiny Falls snatched him and little Axel back here. The strange control of the family or the community, or perhaps both, held them here against my father's will. Now that I was also someone who was snatched and held, I understood.

"I have a job for you, Hayden," Grand-mother said. As was her way, there was no small talk or introduction. But since my long-time best friend Luna was the same way—gosh, I missed her! —I was okay with this abrupt start to our conversation.

"A job? Really?" I asked. Well, that made sense. I was going to live here now, and although I was continuing to run *Natural Living Magazine* with Luna, it wasn't a full-time endeavor. And a job would help me feel I was contributing.

"I have gathered that you are a talented journalist, and your magazine has a healthy following."

"Thank you. And yes, it does."

"I have been contemplating rekindling the Destiny Falls newspaper since our old editor retired. Nowadays most people get their news online, so I would like you to create and run an updated online version of *The Destiny Falls Observer*. With your skills and your tendency toward gossip, this should be a perfect fit for you."

I cringed at the word gossip, but she was entirely correct. The idea excited me! It would provide exactly the credibility I needed to investigate all the secrets of Destiny Falls and its people. My wheels were already turning.

My father stood up at that moment and set a camera down on Grandmother's desk.

"This is the official *Observer* camera," he

said. "It is the only one you should use for photos in the paper."

"I'm going to be taking the photos also?" I asked. "I'm not really a photographer."

"You will be with this camera," my father said.

"Leonard was the *Observer's* photographer while he attended college. He's quite talented, and can teach you all you need to know," my grandmother said. "He can also provide you with past issues and other information to get you started. Please begin immediately."

Grandmother stood up and nodded at both of us. "Good day," she said. Then she walked out of the room. I felt like she should change her exit statement to, "That's all." She reminded me so much of Miranda Priestly from *The Devil Wears Prada*.

"It's a great honor to get to run the *Observer*," my father told me. "You'll get the inside scoop on just about everything, and it opens many doors."

"It sounds right up my alley." It so was! It had been two seconds and already I had a list of articles planned.

"And I'll have the perfect excuse to spend some extra time with my daughter." He gave me a big smile and a thumbs-up. "Do you have time now for me to show you the camera?"

"I have time," I said, "but I've always used my phone. I've got the upgraded camera feature and it takes great shots."

"That may be true," my father said, "but this is a very special camera, used only for the *Observer*."

I'd learned that people around here rarely used the word 'magic,' but they often hinted at it in other ways. I had a feeling this might be one of those times.

"By 'very special' do you mean it's enchanted in some way?" I asked him.

"Perhaps." He smiled at my use of the word 'enchanted.' "The camera works differently with each person who uses it, and there is only one user at a time. If someone else tries to use it, they'll find it pretty much functions as an empty box. Here. Let me show you the basic functions. It's user friendly and will adapt to your needs and habits."

Just like many things around here, I found that to be intriguing, but also a little creepy. Creepy or not, having a camera that functioned as a thinking partner would be handy.

My father was correct. It was easy to use, almost as intuitive as using my phone. Strangely, it was already synced to my phone, so my trial photos appeared in my photos in a brand new folder labeled '*Observer.*' If only all electronics were that easy!

"Leonard!" Grandmother's scream broke through our conversation. It bellowed through the house as if on a loudspeaker, "Call 911. Come outside!"

The two of us sprinted through the house. My father called for emergency help as he ran.

We burst through the front door to see the mail delivery truck in the driveway. The mail carrier was lying on the pavement and pieces of mail were scattered around the yard. The carrier was moaning so, thankfully, he was alive. I didn't think I could handle another dead body. Ouch, that thought sounded self-centered. Of course, I felt bad for this injured person.

I looked down and noticed that my new camera was around my neck, but I knew for sure that I didn't put it there. I took that as a sign and snapped a few quick photos.

I could already hear the ambulance driving our way. In just minutes, they were tending to the injured mail carrier, putting him on a stretcher, and driving away to the hospital. I barely had time to process the event, and it seemed to be over.

My father picked up the pieces of mail, which all appeared to be addressed to Caldwell residents. The keys were still in the mail truck, and one of the maintenance staff pulled it over near the garage.

We were all heading back into the house when a FedEx van pulled up to the house. The carrier handed a box to Leonard, got his signature, and drove off.

Leonard examined the package with a puzzled look. "Hayden, this is for you."

12

A package for me? My father handed it over. It was large and heavy. I glanced at the return label. 'Destiny Falls Ferry System.' My brain pinged and my first thoughts were of Nakita, the ferry captain, saying, "I have something for you," "tell no one," "for the safety of your family," and "life or death."

I quickly corralled my thoughts. "Oh, my order arrived!" I lied. "I think I'll go unpack it." I turned away, heading off any questions. I went into the house, struggling to carry the heavy box up to my room. My father offered to help, but I yelled, "Got it!" over my shoulder.

My door shut behind me more loudly than I intended. I placed the box on my floor and stared at it. My breathing was coming out fast and loud, my heart was thumping.

"Whoa, Nelly. Is that a box of snakes or something?" Latifa and Chanel were creeping cautiously toward the box and eyeing it as if something would pop out at any moment.

"This is from the ferry company. I think it might be what Nakita, the ferry captain, was planning to give me."

"You mean the lady who is . . . dearly departed?" She whispered the words 'dearly de-

parted.'

I nodded. The three of us just stared at the box. Finally, Chanel broke the silence with a meow. Latifa translated, *"She thinks you should open it."*

The two of them backed up a few feet and huddled close together.

I grabbed a pair of scissors off my desk and sat down on the floor next to the box. I scored along the tape lines, then pulled the box open.

It was a mess. It looked like a toddler had packed it. I dug through it and saw documents, receipts, ledgers, notebooks, and file folders. Many of the papers were wrinkled or creased. The box was filled to capacity.

"This is bizarre," I said. "I wonder if this is what someone thought was in the mail truck?"

"What mail truck?" asked Latifa.

I realized that the cats had been upstairs and missed the drama of the injured postal worker and the mail strewn all over the yard. I shared the story and they agreed it seemed connected.

"Well, I'm due over at Olivia's for lunch," I said. I lugged the box into my closet and covered it with my stack of laundry to make it less conspicuous. "I'll look through this tonight."

"Before you abandon us. Yet again." Deep sigh. *"What's with the camera around your neck?"*

I gave the cats a quick rundown of my new job as editor and photographer for the *Destiny Falls Observer*. They were duly impressed.

"It wouldn't hurt you to practice using it,"

Latifa said as she began to pose.

When we finished her impromptu modeling session, I turned on the movie channel and filled the cat food bowl. I grabbed the box of blueberry scones I had picked up from Vessie's café for Olivia.

Latifa made a coughing noise.

"What?"

"Are those bluuueberry scones? Ah, how I love bluuueberry scones," she said.

"Have you ever had blueberry scones?"

"No. But I loooove them."

I put a few pieces on a small plate for them to share, then headed out to my friend's home for a visit and lunch.

Olivia and Hercules were enjoying the beautiful day out on her porch. She waved happily as I approached. Of course, there was a fresh pitcher of lemonade and a platter of homemade cookies on the table, along with an assortment of sandwiches, olives, and pickles. I lifted the box from Vessie's and waved it at her.

"Ohhh. I know that's going to be good! I love Vessie's treats," Olivia said. She took the box and peeked in, sniffing and moaning. "Yum. Scones! Thanks, Hayden."

"You're welcome. Thank you for inviting me to lunch."

Hercules lumbered over to me in his half-asleep state and yawned, showing off his massive doggie teeth. Then he leaned his body into mine, looked up with puppy-dog eyes, and waited to be stroked.

"You silly boy," I said. "You love your rubs, don't you?" I didn't even have to bend over to pet him; his head was at the level of my elbow. I reached into my pocket and pulled out the baggie of meat I had brought for him. He eagerly but gently took it out of my hand, then returned to his corner to continue his nap.

We sat at the table and filled our plates, enjoying what I knew was warm-up small talk. Olivia always had local news and gossip to share and I looked forward to it.

"Want to tell me about your new camera?" She pointed down to the case next to my feet.

And there sat the camera case that I had not brought with me to Olivia's. It seemed I now had both a talking cat and a sidekick camera.

"I have a new job!" I told Olivia. "Eleanor asked me to create and manage an online version of the old *Destiny Falls Observer*."

"Eleanor *asked* you? That doesn't sound like the Eleanor I know," she chuckled.

"Okay, fine. She *directed* me to create the paper and to be the photographer, too. This is my unique work camera."

"And by unique, you mean charmed?" Olivia tilted her chin toward the camera bag. "You seemed just as surprised as I was to see it appear next to you."

"Exactly right. Apparently, my father used to be the photographer for the paper, so he's going to be giving me some guidance."

"Sounds like a pleasant way to get to know each other," she said. Olivia had quickly become a trusted friend, so she knew much of the story of my whirlwind month.

"I loved that old paper. Used to read it in the morning with my tea. It featured only local news, so none of that stressful politics and world affairs." She waved her hands in the air. "Too much of that can cause heartburn."

I agreed with her. And it was nice to know the expectation would be local news only. That I could wrap my arms around.

"You heard about the ferry captain?" I asked her. Of course she had. I wanted to open that topic and find out what she knew. I wondered if this story should be in the *Observer*. I'd have to discuss the parameters with Grandmother or my father.

"That's such a shame. So sad." She paused just long enough to make it a polite statement, then launched into her gossip. "There was always something off about her. Not that it excuses murder, of course," Olivia said.

"What do you mean something was off?"

"I often saw her hanging around with the guy that drives the boat and two of the mechanics."

"You mean Kerbie, the helmsman?" I asked.

"Oh! You know Kerbie?"

"Not really. I met him at Vessie's once. Just briefly. Saw him with two really large men who looked like mechanics."

"Yep. They're mechanics." Olivia tried to stifle a laugh. "I've only ever heard them called Gronk and Shrek. I don't know if that's their real names though."

"Very fitting," I agreed. "They're quite a trio. All three rotund guys, but Kerbie being so short with his bright red hair, and the two of them looking like black-haired giants next to him."

"They always seemed to be off in a corner, secluded and anti-social. And they entered the ferry building from the back door, away from all the passengers."

"I've seen passengers going to the back door," I said. "They were dressed for skiing, which seemed odd. They came back around, and it appeared they were holding tickets."

"Hmm. That is odd," she said. Now, she wasn't fooling me. Olivia knew everything, yet she sometimes kept details to herself. Typically, given time, these seeped out a little at a time.

"How did girls' night go with your sisters?" Olivia asked, deftly changing the subject. I couldn't help it. I started chattering about my wonderful time with the girls, gushing about sisterhood. "We talked some about my mother. It was nice. We finished off a blender of margaritas, and they let it slip that my father never got over his love for her."

Olivia was nodding with a sad look on her face. "And Emily has never gotten over him, either," she said.

"What?" I said.

"What?" she said back. Then she abruptly stood up and grabbed the lemonade pitcher and announced it needed a refill.

"Wait, Olivia. Do you know my mother?"

But she was scurrying into the house. I followed her into the kitchen.

"Olivia? Were you friends with my mother?"

"Did you want more lemonade?" She acted as if I hadn't spoken.

"Olivia? You said something about my mother."

"You must have misunderstood me," she said. "More cookies, too?"

I knew I had not misunderstood her. As much as a gossip as she was, Olivia appeared to know exactly how to keep a secret.

Suddenly, Hercules began barking in the back yard. Hercules was an incredibly well-trained dog and he was usually quiet. I had rarely heard him bark. He didn't bark at random things like squirrels or a car driving by, so we knew it was something to investigate. We went out the back door to find out what the commotion was about.

Hercules had his nose in a bush. His tail was wagging happily, and his bark was excited. He ran and forth between us and the bushes, clearly telling Olivia to look there.

Olivia and I carefully eased the branches aside and there, at the base of a tree, was the tiniest little black kitten. It looked up at us with big, sad eyes and mewed pitifully.

"Oh my stars!" gushed Olivia.

We both crouched down and looked at the tiny creature. Hercules barked again from where he was standing, about twenty feet away from us. Olivia walked over, then told me not to come. In a quiet voice, like she was trying not to let the kitten hear her, she told me that it appeared a coyote has gotten to the mother cat.

I carefully scooped up the little bundle of black fur. The kitten was trembling.

"You poor little baby," I said. The kitten seemed to melt into the warmth and security of my arms. I carried her to the front porch and fed her bits of tuna from my sandwich. She seemed ravenous. I wondered how long she'd been hiding in the bushes.

"Do you mind if I take this little bundle home with me?" I asked Olivia. "I already have cat supplies, plus two furry companions."

"That's a lovely idea," she agreed.

13

No one was home to see me sneak upstairs with my tiny little bundle of black fur. I was glad, as I wasn't sure if this was going to be okay with the family. I mean, everyone seemed to welcome Latifa into the house, but would they also accept a new kitten?

I hoped that Latifa and Chanel would be okay with a new feline addition to the household. I figured Latifa would be, since she was cool with new adventures. I didn't know Chanel all that well, and there was none of that telepathic communication between us. Latifa had translated everything I knew about her; it wasn't firsthand. This house had been Chanel's domain, and she was accustomed to being the Big Cat on Campus. I suspected that she accepted Latifa so easily because they were two of a kind. Smart, sassy movie buffs with a love of sneaking out to the great outdoors and napping on silk pillows in the sunshine. They were clearly meant to be, and their connection had been immediate. But would Chanel accept a new kitten into her home?

The cats were not in my bedroom, so they were likely snoozing in the sunshine or sneaking around the garden. That was good. I could get this little furball set up before the big reveal. I planned to let the cats help me name the kitten, which Olivia and I determined was a female. Thank you, Google.

I made a soft blanket nest in the middle of the bed and settled the little one into it. I laid down next to her, stroked her soft fur, and listened to her tiny little purr. She tipped over onto her side and began kneading the blanket while she enjoyed being snuggled.

I heard a commotion in my closet, which clearly was a clue to the cats' secret doorway system. A minute later, the two sauntered into the bedroom. They saw me on the bed and jumped up next to me.

"A kitten!?" Latifa gasped. *"It's a kitten! Why do you have a kitten?!"*

"Hercules found her today, in Olivia's backyard. She was hidden in the bushes. Clearly starving and frightened."

The kitten softly mewed and looked up intently at the two big cats, her bright, emerald green eyes taking measure of these creatures.

The two cats crowded into my space, effectively pushing me aside with their substantial backsides. They were rubbing their faces on her cheeks, mewing and licking her soft fur.

I enjoyed watching the two of them instantly turn into mamas right there in front of me.

"I figured you two could help me name her," I said.

"Lola," said Latifa.

"Hmm. I like that. It's a good possibility." I nodded.

"No, Ace. Not asking your opinion. Her name is Lola."

"How do you know?" The kitten had no collar or tag.

"She just told us," said Latifa.

I quietly watched while Latifa and Chanel got to know our sweet little Lola. After a while, Chanel picked her up by the scruff and the three of them jumped off the bed and moved to the private cat alcove that was near my closet. Clearly, I had just helped create a lovely new family.

I left the cats alone and used the rest of the evening to catch up on my work and to e-mail Luna, Nana, and Granana. I snuck into the yoga room three times to peek in the teardrop mirror. I noticed the shape has changed, and it was now an oval. But it was simply a mirror. I only saw the yoga room reflected back at me. I would keep checking. I knew the mirror was a key to connecting with my family back home. I just needed to be patient and let it unfold.

My phone pinged and I smiled when I saw a text from Axel.

*You up for breakfast with Jax
& me at Vessie's tomorrow at 7?*

Yes! Would love that. :)

Busy day, so we'll have to drive.

Sounds good. See you in the morning.

I was feeling hungry and thought I'd trek downstairs for a sandwich. I opened my door to the hallway to find a gloriously full food cart with an assortment of dinner items. Bless this house. Or Cleobella. Or whoever or however the food appeared. It tickled me to see a tiny cat toy resting in a small ceramic bowl that said '*Welcome*' across the front. Clearly, that was for our new arrival.

As I was getting ready for bed, I heard Latifa's voice coming from the cat alcove. She was crooning a sweet-sounding lullaby. My hands went to my heart and I felt a surge of love for my suddenly maternal pet.

I snuck a little closer and put my ear to the opening, and then I heard what she was singing:

"Well, I'm not the world's most passionate guy,
But when I looked in her eyes,
Well, I almost fell for my Lola
L-O-L-A. Lola, lo lo lo lo Lola . . .
She . . . umm. Somethin' Somethin' champagne.
Like Coca Cola…. C-O-L-A Cola. Lo lo lo lo Lola…."

14

For the first time, in a long time, I woke up without my furry companion squashed up next to me or sprawled over the top of me. Instead, I had three furry companions curled up in a heap a foot away from me on the bed. Since they were snuggled up in their own little pile, I had a blissful few inches of space all to myself.

What a colorful blend of softness they made—the rich chocolate points of my Himalayan, the brilliant white of Chanel, the magnificent Persian, and the tiny little spot of black fuzz tucked between them. I reached over for my phone and snapped a picture. I snuck out of bed very quietly, because, well, they had a busy day ahead. All those important meetings to attend today, right? Okay, not meetings. Snacks, catnip, and naps. Even so, one did not disturb sleeping babies, cats, or dogs.

Why do people tiptoe? I wondered. It really does not make them any quieter. I did it anyway, and made my way across the room to peek into my yoga room—nope, nothing in the mirror this morning—and then to my bathroom to get ready for my breakfast with Axel and Jaxson.

It was still early, and the mystery box beckoned. With a half hour before I needed to meet up with the guys, I had time to start looking through the mess of documents. I shoved aside the pile of clothes covering the box and opened it up.

At first glance, it appeared that someone had upended an entire file cabinet into the box. Papers, files, and notecards were heaped in random order. An assortment of paper clips, pens, rubber bands, loose change, and postage stamps was shoved in between the other things.

What would probably make the most sense would be to sort through the items and put similar things together. I could sort the paperwork and files and place everything right-side up. Then I would get a better sense of what I was looking at. Not enough time to start that now.

As I closed the box and piled my laundry over the top of it, something dawned on me. Olivia had said that Nakita was friends with Kerbie. Shrek, and Gronk. Then why did she act so anxious when she saw the mechanics walk into the café? If they were friends, why the cause for concern? Maybe something in this box would provide clues. It would have to wait for later, though, since it was time to meet up with Axel and Jax.

I left the kitty-pile still sweetly asleep on my bed and slipped out into the hallway. There it was, right across from my room, in its usual morning spot. The anthropomorphized traveling window seat enjoying the early morning sunshine for its own snooze. I noticed the bookshelf was rearranged and now also contained several vases of fresh flowers set between the books for a very pretty effect. I'd need to check it out later to determine if any new books were added. The window seat library yielded some very enlightening books about Destiny Falls and the Caldwell family. It would also be helpful as I tackled putting together the Destiny Falls online newspaper. I added those things to my growing list of to-dos.

As always, I didn't rush my way through the house. I savored the experience. It seemed the wood railings had been polished because they had a more vivid shine than usual. And that was saying a lot. The beautiful woods throughout this home were obviously well maintained by someone. Who, I didn't know, as the household staff must have done their work while I was gone or sleeping? Or . . . wait. Did the house maintain itself? That would be very possible. A self-cleaning house. Oh yeah. Package that and I could make a million. Or ten.

I met Axel downstairs in the foyer. My spirits lightened the minute I saw my brother's smiling face. At that moment, our father Leonard came around the corner from the kitchen.

"Good morning, guys," he said, looking quite pleased to be able to say that.

How nice it felt to hear my father say 'guys' and have it mean me and my brother. I bet he felt great joy in that. After a lifetime of having his children separated, to have us all three together was a blessing.

"Hayden, do you have time later this afternoon to go to the newspaper office with me and start your new adventure?"

"Yes! I would love that." I was excited to see what secrets the office might hold. We set a plan to meet up later and Axel and I headed out to meet up with Jaxson.

~ ~ ~

Axel chose a table by the window, and we settled into the pink booth in Vessie's pink café. The flowing lines of butterflies were not decorating the walls today. Instead, the walls were frosted with climbing bougainvillea plants bursting with pink blossoms. The front door was decorated with a white, arched arbor covered with the same plant, plus small, pink, fairy lights. Oh, wait! The butterflies were here! They were just tucked in between the flowers. I could see their gently fluttering wings peeking out here and there. The overall effect was captivating.

"Good morning, friends!" Vessie walked up to our table, drying her hands on a pink towel. I stood up for our requisite hug. I was getting accustomed to the easy affection here. More than that, to be honest. I was enjoying the warm displays that seemed so normal to the people I'd met here.

Today Vessie was dressed in white flowing

trousers and a colorful, embroidered peasant top. Her charming attire blended perfectly with today's décor. "Will it be just the two of you?" she asked.

"Jaxson will be joining us," said Axel.

"Oh, wonderful!" She smiled brightly. "Something to drink while you're waiting?"

"Tea for me, please," I said. Axel ordered a latte and Vessie went off to the counter for our drinks.

Axel looked over my shoulder and his face burst into a smile and he waved. I knew Jaxson had entered the building. They'd been friends since college, but even beyond that, there was something magnetic about Jax. He glowed with personality. His three-day stubble and just-a-bit-too-long hair gave a relaxed vibe that balanced with his strong, muscular body. When he saw me, he bestowed me with that Matthew McConaughey smile, dimples and all, that made me weak. The way he looked at me spoke volumes. It brought back my vision from the falls and my suspicion that he might be the man of my future.

Jaxson sat down next to me and looked deep into my eyes as he said good morning. I was enveloped in the musky scent of Armani cologne. He was bewitching.

I didn't know him well, as all of our encounters had revolved around murder cases, Jeep break-ins, and assault cases. I had held back on pursuing anything more since I had just been a visitor in Destiny Falls. But now that it appeared I was here to stay, maybe it was time to get to know him on a more personal level. Based on his intimate smiles, perhaps he felt the same.

Vessie reappeared at the table with our beverages and said hello to Jaxson. He stood up, took her hands, and smiled that Matthew McConaughey smile, dimples and all, as he looked deep into her eyes and said good morning. Well, hmm. Perhaps his charm wasn't reserved exclusively for me. Now that the stars in my eyes began to dim, I realized he'd been every bit as charismatic with just about anyone I'd seen him with. Unless he was working, then he was All Sheriff, All Business. Which was sexy in a whole different way. That didn't mean he wasn't The Future Husband and Father of my Future Children, but I'd take this slowly and see where it went. After all, there was obviously more than one man who fit the character in my vision.

Our breakfast visit was delightful. I enjoyed spending time with my brother and his buddy, mystery man or not. After we ate, we ordered another round of coffee and tea, and Jaxson filled us in on the latest in the murder of the ferry captain.

"We're making headway on the case," Jaxson began.

Wow, this I wanted to hear. I'd been mulling over my unsettling encounter with the captain, her message, the strange men in the café, and the mystery package. Because of her dire warnings, I didn't want to be the one to share these facts and possibly endanger myself or my family.

"We've learned that Nakita was in the process of a contentious divorce. Apparently, she'd been having an affair. Her husband discovered it and he was furious. We're trying to locate her husband and also identify the man she was having the affair with. It's been a challenge. Both men have been evasive, but we have some leads that we're working through. We suspect this was a crime of passion."

Wait. What?! This was not at all what I was expecting to hear. What about her odd behavior? Her warning in the café? The intimidating mechanics? The package? This was not adding up.

"Hayden, are you okay?" Axel's voice made its way through my fog.

"Oh. Yeah. Sorry. Just processing." I was way more than processing. I was panicking. *What should I do now? Should I tell them about the box? About my encounter with Nakita? About my suspicions about the mechanics?*

I excused myself to use the restroom and stood there trying to think but finding it hard to do so around the buzzing going on in my brain. Nakita's 'life or death' warning had proved to be accurate in that she was now, as Latifa would say, dead. And the postal worker had been accosted and the Caldwell mail ransacked right before I received the FedEx package. This wasn't a situation to be taken lightly. I paced back and forth in the tiny room and finally decided I would mention a few vague details and see if Jaxson would take these and proceed with an eye to something nefarious.

I sat back down in the booth. "There are a few things you should know," I said, treading lightly. "I met Nakita in line at the café a couple of days before her death."

Both men turned to look at me, their expectant expressions making me sweat.

"She seemed nervous. Two men in ferry uniforms, who looked like mechanics, came in after she did. She appeared to mistrust them."

Jaxson took out his phone and made some notes. Good. I could get him started on thinking that there was more to this story.

"Can you describe the men for me?" he asked.

"They were tall and very large, overweight men. Both had black hair. They were wearing ferry uniforms, like coveralls. Both rather dirty, but it looked more like grease; that's why I thought they might be mechanics. I've since learned that they are. I also saw them near the ambulance the day that Nakita's body was removed from the ferry."

"Fits the description of the two mechanics at the scene, name tags said Gronk and Shrek. Easy to remember those two. Was Nakita alone when she came into the café that day?"

"No, she was with Kerbie, the helmsman. They seemed like friendly coworkers. Do you know Kerbie?"

"Perhaps. Can you describe him for me?" Jaxson said.

"He's very short, less than five feet tall. He was also obese. His hair was a very bright red. He was also there at the ambulance, standing near the stretcher."

Jaxson nodded. "Yes, that's the helmsman. Is there anything else of significance from the day you met her?" he asked.

Boy, the million-dollar question. I took a sip of my tea to hide my face and shook my head. "I think that's pretty much all of it for now." I'd never been a liar, so concealing my encounter with her made me uncomfortable. I hoped they would move on with the conversation. Which they did. Thankfully.

I felt like I'd been holding my breath since breakfast with Jaxson and Axel. Now that I was back in my room, I let out a tremendous sigh and dropped into a chair.

There was a scuffle behind me. I turned to see Latifa and Chanel playing with Lola. I use the word 'playing' loosely. The kitten was so full of energy, she was all over the place. I laughed at Latifa and Chanel. They were sprawled on their sides— the only thing moving was their front paws. They were batting cat toys back and forth for Lola to chase. She would pounce on a feathered toy and then jump onto one of the big cats, then back again, chasing the toy. Latifa and Chanel both looked exhausted.

"Welcome to motherhood, ladies," I said.

15

I had a few hours before meeting my father at the *Destiny Falls Observer* office, so I decided to hike through Twin Falls Park and take some photos with my new camera.

The park was amazing. It was more like a forest than a park, really. Luckily, there was a maze of trails made of wood chips or gravel, so it was quite a pleasant, easy trek. The abundance of vegetation and wildlife made it a virtual photographer's paradise. I was so intent on taking a photo of a butterfly that had landed on a flowering bush that I never heard someone approach behind me.

"That's a pretty butterfly," the voice whispered.

"Oh!" My jerk and yelp scared the butterfly away.

I looked up to see Han standing behind me. All decked out for a day on the trails.

"You startled me!"

"Oops," said Han. "I should have said boooo!" He raised his hands and wiggled his fingers in a menacing way. We both laughed.

"I should know better," he said. "I'm an amateur wildlife photographer, myself. Sorry for interfering with your shot."

"That's okay. I'm just getting comfortable

with my new camera."

"Taking up a new hobby, are you?" Han asked.

"Not a hobby. A new job! My grandmother has asked me to start up the *Destiny Falls Observer* as an online paper."

"Eleanor *asked* you?" he laughed. Clearly, anyone who knew my grandmother knew she was much more direct than that.

"Okay, fine. She assigned me a new job. Editor *and* photographer. I'll be meeting my father at the newspaper office in a bit, so I thought I'd get comfortable with the equipment."

"How's it going? Need any help?" he offered. "I'm not a pro, but I can make my way around the basics."

"Actually, yes. I'm having a bit of trouble with the close-up focus. That's why I was working on the butterfly."

"Yeah, focus can be a frustrating element until you master it. Want to show me your shots?"

Han and I spent the next two hours together. He had enough knowledge about cameras to help me figure out some details. True to my father's comment, if Han tried to take a photo to demonstrate something, the result was an empty black square. Being a Destiny Falls native, an enchanted camera didn't faze him. He just shrugged it off and changed his approach to showing me what to do and then letting me take the photos. This required close contact, as we both hovered over the camera. When he touched my hand to guide me on a setting, or when I felt his breath on me as he explained a detail, it was as if there was an invisible connection between us. It wasn't that crazy zap I'd heard about in romance novels; it was more a deep-rooted bond being awakened.

When I first met Han a month ago, I was bowled over by his smoldering good looks and smooth James Bond-ish personality. Over time, I learned that he was one of those rare, gorgeous guys who was even more incredible on the inside than the outside. He was kind, polite, and easy to be around. He made me laugh and he paid attention when I talked. Even more, he seemed interested in the same kinds of things that I liked, and he laughed with gusto over my jokes. When he had shared his feelings about his affection for his sisters, that cemented his position as utterly endearing.

"Look!" He got my attention and pointed up.

There was an owl up in the tree not far from us. I'd never seen an owl here, though I had heard them quite a few times. We quietly inched closer, and I took several splendid pictures.

"Wow! So glad you saw him," I said. "Must be your keen investigator's eye."

"Yeah. Coz you have to keep an eye out for those crafty, nocturnal birds of prey." He gifted me with his wide smile, his eyes twinkling.

I was melting into his gaze when I was suddenly jolted into reality. "Oh shoot! I have to go meet my father at the newspaper office. And I'm keeping you from your hike!"

"Hayden, spending time with you has been more rewarding than any hike I could have taken."

I felt the heat creep up my face and I stammered some reply. I couldn't even understand what I said. Being as sweet as he is, he just let that go and helped me pack up my camera.

"Today's just my warm-up hike," Han said. "Day after tomorrow, I'm planning a trek up to the lake at the top."

"That sounds wonderful! I'm looking forward to making that hike again. In the meantime, I have a new job to learn!"

Han wished me good luck for the day with a soft kiss on my cheek, then hiked off in the direction he was heading originally. My hand came up to touch the place he'd kissed, and I had a warm feeling as I watched him walk away. He seemed like the real deal, this one.

16

Eleanor had explained that the newspaper editor retired months ago, but the newspaper office had remained intact. They were hoping to get it up and running again, and it contained all the old physical copies in storage, so they felt it valuable to keep things as they were. The office was in one of the Caldwell buildings, and I was delighted to discover that it was just down the block from Poppy's Extravaganza and only a short walk from Vessie's Café.

The building ran the length of the block and contained three businesses: a clothing boutique on one end, an antique shop on the other, and the *Observer* office in the middle. It was a single-story building made of brick but was designed with about six different shades of red, gold, and brown bricks in a friendly pattern, making it look fresh and modern. There were hanging baskets dripping with flowers, and a striped awning over the entire length of the building that gave it a jaunty, Hallmark, small-town feel. There was a white-painted bench set out front, next to a large pot of flowers, and a colorful flag waving in the breeze. I loved it at first sight.

The bench was so welcoming, I took a seat there to wait for my father. It gave me an opportunity to absorb all the businesses surrounding my new workplace. I spotted a wide range of shops including a flower shop, a pharmacy, and an art gallery. There was a small park in the space between some shops, with a picnic table that looked like a great place to have lunch.

It was so quiet here. Nothing like the bustle of Seattle. I had nothing against bustle, of course. But the peacefulness here was refreshing. It felt honest.

"Hey there, Hayden." My father's voice broke the silence. He sat down beside me on the bench. "Sorry I'm late."

"Oh, are you late? I thought I was early."

He looked at his phone. "Yep. I guess you are early, and so am I." He handed me a key ring with several keys on it and motioned grandly to the front door. "Welcome to your new kingdom. Ready to go inside?"

"Very ready!" I got up and unlocked the door, eager to step inside.

The newspaper office was so much nicer than I had expected. I was picturing an old-time printing press, black file cabinets, ugly yellow lighting, and messy brown desks. Clearly, I'd seen too many old movies. I could thank Latifa for that. Instead, it was a bright, open space dotted with comfortable furniture and three clean, modern desks. Two of the desks were empty, but the third held a computer with several large monitors and a desktop printer.

It seemed a comfortable size for three or four people to work here. I assumed the editor was the only full-time person, but we hadn't discussed that. How many people did it take to run a small community newspaper? I had no idea. But now that it would be digital, I suspected that I could manage on my own.

There was a wall filled with special wooden filing cabinets that had wide, shallow drawers that obviously fit the newspapers. Several bookcases held directories and research books.

There were photos displayed on the walls that appeared to be those from the paper. Gorgeous shots of the parks, waterfalls, shops, and the ferry. There were portrait-quality shots of the local people and events.

Large windows made up the entire front of the space, providing a splendid view of the shops across the road. The back appeared to have a bathroom and a door leading out to the alley behind the building.

The atmosphere hummed with years of memories and windows to the past. I could almost feel the history in here amongst the old papers, books, and the photographs. Soft cciling lighting made the room glow golden, and I noticed beautiful, antique desk lamps on each working space. I felt the promise of future memories brewing. The space reminded me of a cozy library, one of my favorite places. I instantly felt at home.

"Is there an offset printing press in here?" I

asked.

"No big equipment here," my father answered. "We outsourced the print runs. Though since you'll be fully online, you won't need to worry about that."

My father pointed to the newspaper filing drawers. "You'll find the most recent year filed out here, and older years in the back room. As you can see, there's also a wide variety of research books on local topics plus area maps and business information."

That was very interesting, and an unexpected perk. As soon as he said that I was itching to scan those shelves. And he did say maps. Perhaps I'd finally unravel the mystery of our exact location and learn the layout of the islands surrounding us.

Over the next hour, my father walked me through the office and chatted with me about the paper. He suggested I read through some recent past issues to get a sense of what news had typically been covered in the paper. Well, he didn't have to ask me twice.

My father finished up the tour and description of the job and then left for another appointment. I had plenty of time before tonight's family dinner to explore, and I fully intended to make the most of every moment. Putting my hands on my hips, I surveyed the room. It would take days to acclimate. Where should I start? I had a hard time deciding between the research books and the old newspapers, but I began with the last of the printed issues.

Precise labeling on the drawers was a good sign. Whoever had worked here before had liked things orderly.

The drawer with the final issues from six months ago was front and center. I pulled out the last few issues. The paper wasn't printed in big-city size. It was more like an oversized magazine. The paper had been published monthly. The sections were specific and organized—news, local events, sports, community announcements, food, entertainment, real estate, deaths and births, and a spotlight feature of one resident or business. They sprinkled it with ads from local businesses and event notices. On my next visit here, I'd read through some issues and maybe take a few of them home.

This project was totally do-able, particularly since it would be fully online. I opened a note page and began organizing a checklist:

Create a website and subscriber sign-up page.

Contact businesses who advertised previously—ask for ads.

Locate past subscriber list. Send an introductory note and sign-up info.

Reach out to local schools, theaters, clubs, churches for community notices.

Find out if there is a local government office —Mayor? City council?

Notify local funeral homes and maternity wards/birth centers/midwives.

Get a list of all local businesses.

Create mock-up for online format; choose and announce first issue date.

Meet with Eleanor regarding expectations/update.

I knew that the set-up and the first few issues would be the hardest. Man, I wished I had Luna as a partner on this. She was brilliant at organization. Not to mention, I missed the heck out of her. I was still holding onto the hope that the mirror was a way to connect with her and my family.

I felt like I had a plan now. Once I got the ball rolling, it should be straightforward. I stood at the door, ready to leave, and scanned my new domain. I felt a tingle of excitement that I couldn't contain. My squeal of delight burst out into the quiet space. I was glad I didn't have an audience for that. This was going to be a fantastic opportunity; I could feel it.

17

Family dinner night around here was either a stuffy, boring event or a three-ring circus. I didn't know which this evening would hold. I had been told that we'd be in the dining room, which was nice. I loved the outdoor events just as much, but I enjoyed the warmth and intimacy of the grand dining space in the home. One wouldn't normally use both grand and intimate at the same time to describe a place, but that was true here. The ski lodge/cabin décor was warm and inviting, but the size of the space was vast. There were sparkling chandeliers dropping from incredibly high ceilings, set off by the tallest rock fireplace that soared all the way up. There was a unique combination of magnificent yet homey here at Caldwell Crest.

I'd been planning to tell the family about Lola tonight, and hopefully, they'd welcome the kitten into the family. She had quickly found her way into my heart. Clearly, Latifa and Chanel had already bonded with her and had morphed right into the motherhood role.

The minute I stepped into the dining room, it was clear I needn't have worried. There was an enormous banner slung across the back wall that announced, '*Welcome Lola!*' There were balloons and streamers all around. They were covered with sparkles, so I had a feeling Cleobella—the queen of sparkles—was behind the decorations.

The dining room table was enormous today. The size changed depending on the number of guests, and a quick count showed about a dozen places set at the table. I guessed welcoming a new kitten was a reason to gather. This family never ceased to amaze me. They'd seem all stuffy and formal and then turn around and put on a party for a little, black, fluffball.

I looked up to see my sister Indigo coming into the dining room. Her husband, Omar, and his brother, Dante, along with their two kids were right behind her. The kids were wearing headbands with cat ears, and they were each carrying a small gift, wrapped in paper covered with colorful cats.

I walked over to say hello and leaned down to kid-level. "Hi guys. I love your ears! Did you bring presents for Lola?"

They both nodded. Ian seemed to be more comfortable around me, and that brought out his chatterbox side. "We have cat toys for the kitty! Where's the kitty, Hayden?"

"I don't know, Ian. We must watch for her. She's really little, so if you see her you tell me, okay?"

He said okay, and then he and Tiana ran off and began looking around the room for the kitten.

"They're going to love the kitten," I said to

the adults.

"Yeah, and so will we," said Indigo. "I understand you're the one that found her?"

"Actually, it was Hercules who found her. I was at Olivia's at the time. The kitten was orphaned and hiding in a bush. She was so tiny and alone, I just had to bring her home."

"Good for you," said Omar. "Abandoned kittens deserve a safe place, and a pet can always brighten a home."

Well, I'd be darned! Omar was an animal lover! And he was conversing with me. He'd always been so quiet and stiff before. It was so nice that both he and Ian seemed to be warming up to me. That made me happy. I was feeling more like family all the time.

I was chatting with the group when Sapphire and Axel came in. I was absolutely delighted to see that each of them was bearing a gift for the kitten. Sapphire had a small package, but I could barely see Axel's head behind the rather large cat pillow he was carrying. Watching him struggle with the huge, soft pillow caused the conversation to pause while we all laughed. No one offered to help, as it was just too entertaining. Following the new trend of each cat having a pillow to match their eyes, this one was emerald green. Axel placed it down near the fireplace and turned around to show off his pride by flexing his biceps, which just reignited more laughter. He came over to join our conversation. He stood next to me and leaned his elbow on my shoulder in an affectionate brother-sister pose. If I hadn't said it enough already, I loved having this brother!

If I thought the pillow was a surprise, I looked up to see my father and grandfather carrying in a four-foot-tall cat condo with a scratching post, several hideouts, and a couple of built-in toys. One look at this kitty mansion and I knew Latifa would be green with envy. I'd have to remind her that she got an entire cat alcove when she moved into the house, complete with everything she needed to make her happy, and then some. She didn't get a sparkly banner, though, so I was sure I'd hear about that oversight.

I was soaking up the camaraderie of my new family when the matriarch entered the room. Everyone snapped to attention and minded their manners as soon as Eleanor was around. My grandmother was a force to be reckoned with. She was fully aware of her effect on people, and I suspected she relished having that. She wasn't the least bit afraid to use that power, either.

She looked over at the group of us and I could almost feel the collective intake of breath. And then she smiled at us. It was a rare and beautiful sight, and I knew every one of us felt its glow.

"Hello, children," she said. That might have offended some people in their twenties, but the way she said it enveloped all of us in a bubble of affection that made us feel loved and cared for. It was nice.

"Oh, look," Grandmother said. "Our little guest of honor has arrived."

We all turned toward the door to see Lola, Chanel, and Latifa enter the room. All of them held their heads high and their tails in the air. It was like a little parade of fluff. I bit the inside of my cheek to prevent myself from laughing. They were so freaking adorable.

The three cats walked over to the fireplace. I heard Chanel meow, and then Lola climbed up onto the new cat pillow. I saw that the color perfectly matched the emerald green of her eyes. The maternal adult cats sat on either side of her, looking proud and happy.

Ian and Tiana squealed with delight and ran over to pet the cats and play with the kitten. Everyone commented on how precious Lola was, and then the adults sat at the table for dinner. I noticed that no one forced the children to abandon their post at the cat pillow, and I thought that was super nice.

Wine glasses were already set up and we toasted the new family member and enjoyed a few minutes of casual conversation. Then one of my favorite people to see entered the room with a cart of appetizers. Cleobella had arrived.

Today she was a vision in emerald green, in a nod to Lola's splendid eye color, I assumed. Her dress was a smooth, silk sheath that looked like it has been sewn on her. She was wearing sparkly, white opera gloves that came all the way up past her elbows. Her fingers were adorned with brilliant emerald rings.

She had painted her eyes in shades of green eye shadow in an exaggerated cats-eye design with an explosion of false eyelashes in black and silver that came up and over her expertly tweezed eyebrows. Her shoes were black with towering, thin metallic heels. How on earth she walked on those, let alone served a meal, was a mystery to me. Of course, her gorgeous, white-blond hair was twisted into an elegant chignon. A green and black hat, adorned with feathers and glitter, tilted fashionably on the top of her head.

Cleobella was like a fascinating storybook every time she entered a room, and she never ceased to keep me enthralled. The rest of the family never batted an eye at her wardrobe. Though, I supposed, they'd seen her so many times over the years they had become accustomed to the sight. I hoped I never would.

She caught my eye, and I knew she saw me examining her outfit, so I gave her a big smile and a thumbs-up. She blushed prettily and smiled back. We'd come a long way in our odd friendship, and I enjoyed her presence. Since she neither spoke nor could hear, we had developed a very rudimentary form of sign language, and she was excellent at interpreting my oddly childish motions. When I had time, I was going to look for some YouTube videos and learn some basic sign language. Or maybe I'd ask Grandmother to teach me since I now knew she was an expert at it. I chuckled at that thought, but who knew? Maybe she would tutor me.

Whoever cooked our dinner—Cleobella or the mystery chef I'd never seen?—wanted to uphold the cat theme. We had a generous salad of fresh greens. Some looked shockingly like grass but tasted like sweet lettuce, and she served a pile of it to the cats. The main course was grilled salmon, wild rice, and vegetables. The cats all received a healthy serving of salmon on small silver plates. After the main course, Cleobella brought out large trays of cheese, fruit, and chocolates; they provided small portions of cheese to the furry partygoers.

Back in my room after dinner, I replayed the memories of the evening. Thinking back to Axel carrying in the big, green cat pillow made me laugh all over again.

I changed into yoga pants and a loose T-shirt. My plan was to spend the rest of the night catching up on my *Natural Living Magazine* work. I'd been slacking in that department, and Luna had been picking up the pieces while I'd been away in 'Denmark.' She never complained and was kindly grateful whenever I did my actual job. She was a genuine friend and a great business partner.

After I finished up my work, I planned to

read through some of the old newspapers. I was looking forward to learning more about the community.

With those thoughts in mind, I went into my yoga room—MY yoga room!—and peeked into the mirror. Expecting no surprises, I just did a quick glance, ready to turn away and get to work. My head snapped back, and I sucked in a breath. I was looking into my old apartment kitchen, now Luna's home, apparently being reflected off the mirrored surface of the microwave control panel. And there was Luna, my dear friend. She was in the kitchen making tea, her ever-present energy obvious in her bouncing, happy movements.

I shouted her name by reflex. The mirrors never worked that way, though. It was visual only. I stepped up close to the mirror and jumped up and down and waved my arms wildly. But Luna wasn't looking in my direction. She was taking a cup and the sugar out of the cabinet and busily focused on her tea-making. I grabbed a yoga towel and waved it like a flag, hoping the movement would catch her eye.

Luna poured the water into her cup, added the tea bag and sugar, and strolled out of the kitchen. I texted her immediately, but it bounced back undelivered.

I felt my eyes fill with tears, and my entire body went weak as I sank down onto the floor. My sadness was so incredibly deep, I could feel it flow over me like a sorrowful wave. I sat for a while, my mind empty except for thoughts of Luna, which led to thoughts of Nana and Granana. My hope was fading.

I pulled myself up off the floor, grabbed a sweater, and headed outside.

I found myself on the bench beside the koi pond in the front garden. I watched the waterfall cascading serenely over the terraced rocks and plantings. I saw, but couldn't enjoy, the enchanting flowers, brilliantly colored fish, and the small bridge gracefully arching over the water. This time, when I felt the tears come, I let them flow. I loved it here, I really did. But I missed my family and friend so much it hurt.

At that moment, I realized how deeply painful it must have been for my father, ripped away from his wife and newborn daughter. As a child, I'd never given it a thought. Growing up, Nana and Gran never talked about it, so it wasn't a part of my life. But now, being here, and not knowing if I would ever be with them again, the pain was so deep, I could feel the heavy weight of it pressing on my chest and my throat tightening with grief.

I was crying then like I hadn't cried since I lost my cat when I was six. Deep sorrow was escaping me in gasping breaths. I was sniffing like the child I had been then when my cat disappeared through the mirror. I didn't know it then, but she had landed in little Axel's room. He had kept the pet until her old age took her from him.

I felt someone sit next to me on the bench. A tissue box was being gently placed on my lap. I looked over to see Cleobella beside me. She was dressed in a relatively normal pair of silk pajamas, and on her feet were, I swear, the same style of feathered, high-heeled slippers that I had seen my grandmother wear the day of their pajama party.

Cleobella tenderly put her arm around my shoulders, and I sank into her and let the tears flow.

18

Yesterday had been a whirlwind. It started with breakfast at Vessie's café with Axel and Jaxson, then my delightful camera work in the park with Han. After that, I'd met my father at the *Observer* office, and then the family dinner cat party. Phew. Oh, and I couldn't forget seeing Luna and my award-winning meltdown at the koi pond with Cleobella.

I hoped that today wouldn't be so extreme, but I was about to do something that just about guaranteed I'd be opening a whole new installment of extreme. I dragged out the mystery box, intending to start unraveling its secrets. I had a sneaking suspicion it might be the proverbial pulling of one sweater thread that unraveled the whole thing, but I couldn't just ignore the elephant in my closet.

Cleaning out drawers, closets, and junk was one of my least favorite things to do, and I avoided it if possible. That's why my kitchen junk drawer usually contained year-old receipts, bread bag ties, old ketchup packets, plastic sporks, and takeout menus. But this box was about more than old menus. It possibly contained clues to the ferry captain's death, the secret she was going to tell me, or the reason she had warned me of danger.

I took stock of the box of items and decided that my original plan of sorting by like-items and putting things right-side-up made the most sense. I started pulling out items and making stacks of file folders, loose papers, envelopes, and small pieces of notepaper and index cards. I grabbed a small box from my desk to gather the paper clips, pens, stamps, and other insignificant items.

Now that I was in the process, it really wasn't so bad. I was making good time, spreading things in piles around me on the floor, when I heard a familiar shuffling coming from the closet. It was the telltale sign of cats arriving.

Two seconds later, Lola came bounding through the room—directly through the middle of my piles, knocking everything into one big mess.

"Lola, stop that right now!" Wow, my voice came out sounding just like Nana when I was younger and letting loose too much energy in the house. The difference being, of course, that as a human child I would stop. Since Lola didn't understand English, she continued to pounce and then began batting at the loosely flying papers. It took me just a minute to stand up and scoop her into my arms. I surveyed the mess. She had done a lot of damage in that short blink of time.

"Aww, look at Hayden cuddling our little dumpling," Latifa said, as she and Chanel walked into the room.

I gestured to the floor. "Do you see all the papers here?"

"Yeppers. What cha' up to, Miss Messy-Pants?"

I growled in her direction. Lola reached up and batted at my chin with her tiny, black paw. She looked up at me with wide eyes, no doubt wondering why a human was growling. Eh. How could I stay angry at such an innocent baby? I stroked her soft fur and took a deep breath, then puffed it out with a loud sigh.

Latifa took stock of the room and noticed the FedEx box and its contents strewn all over the floor.

"Ohhh. Hurricane Lola touched down in here, did she?"

"She did. No worries. I'll just start over," I grumbled. "Can you keep her occupied with something else while I work?"

Chanel meowed, and Latifa translated, *"It's naptime now, anyway."* She looked up at Lola. *"Come on, Nugget, time for a nap."*

I gently put the kitten down and stroked her tiny head. "I know you meant no harm, sweetie. Papers are fun to play with, aren't they?" She rubbed her head on my hand and purred. It was nice to have my furry little family of cats. No matter what, I never felt alone.

The three cats made their way into the cat alcove. I noticed there were now three pillows in there. The green and blue ones that matched Lola's and Latifa's eyes, and a new golden, copper-colored one to match Chanel's. I assumed that her pink pillow remained downstairs. How the pillows got here, I had no idea, but Caldwell Crest had a way of taking care of its own. Not that they needed three pillows. They'd all end up in one big bunch on one of them. But it was a sweet gesture, nonetheless.

An hour later I was still sorting through items in the box, but I was almost to the end. As I pulled the last file out, I noticed a yellow post-it note stuck to the bottom. A messy, hastily scribbled note that read: *Hayden—I'm sorry. I tried. Be careful. N.*

It was obvious that N was Nakita. But seriously? *I'm sorry? I tried? Be careful!?* She was just as vague in writing as she had been in person. What was she sorry for? Why was she killed? What did I have to do with all this? Why did she send the box to me? Why had she warned me to tell no one? That my family could be in danger? Did that still apply? She said it was *life or death*—did she mean *her death* or *mine*? My family? And what about the mysterious and dangerous island named Gladstone that she had warned me about? That was still an unknown. Oh my God. My brain was about to explode.

Nakita had sent me the box for a reason. I needed to find out what that reason was. It would make sense that something in here would lead me to answers. I needed to organize the paperwork so I could begin reading through it.

Finally, I had all the items sorted and lined

up vertically in the box. None of them had labels that would enable me to organize them further or to determine the contents. And there was a huge stack of loose papers as well. I'd just have to start at a random beginning and work my way through.

Most of the documents so far had to do with ferry passages. That, of course, made sense. One folder contained ledgers of payments. There were about a dozen pages. The dollar amounts were large—about twenty times what I'd expect a ferry ticket to cost. There were four columns. The first was a list of names—printed and then signed. The second column was labeled *Approved or Denied*. The last two columns were filled in for all names, regardless of approved or denied. One column labeled *Agent* had one initial of A, K, or V. The final column was labeled *Paid*, and it also had one initial, either L or M. Oddly enough, nothing was dated.

It was strange that these ledgers were all written by hand. In today's world, who kept handwritten ledgers? The excessive dollar amounts clearly were not for ferry tickets, unless the ferry was also used as a cruise ship! Which, I supposed, would be possible here in Destiny Falls. But there were no other indications of that. People going on and off the ferry never gave me a cruise-ship or lengthy voyage type of vibe.

I picked up the next file. It contained more of the ledgers showing the exact same format. Another dozen or so of them.

I stood up and stretched. I'd have a cup of tea and then continue going through the files.

There was a sound outside my door, and I opened it an inch and peeked out. The window seat had moved to be directly across from my door. The familiar tea cart was there, with a steaming fresh pot of tea and a platter of cookies and tiny muffins. I opened the door fully and looked both ways. No one. Whether Cleobella, the window seat, the house, or the town had created these magical little perks was a puzzle. On one hand, it was nice to find these surprises. On the other hand, well, it was just a little bit creepy. Kind of like when ads for shoes showed up on my phone an hour after I've been looking at black leather pumps.

Creepy or not, I took it as a sign to take a break from the files, have some tea, and browse the window seat bookcase for any new books.

I poured a cup of tea, took a bite of a warm chocolate chip cookie—yum!—and scanned the bookshelves. One book title caused me to drop my cookie right into my teacup, and it landed with a splash. The title of the book was *Gladstone*.

19

The splashed tea and crumpled cookie were totally forgotten while I reached up and took down the book entitled *Gladstone*. The full title on the cover was *Gladstone: Past, Present, and Myths*. There was a stamped banner across the cover that said: *Destroy Copy*. I sat on the cushioned seat and warily opened the book.

The inside cover was a map! It too carried the *Destroy Copy* stamp, but I could see enough through the words. The map showed the cluster of nearly a hundred islands, just as I had seen on the enchanted globe in the library. I located the crescent-shaped island labeled *Destiny Falls*, and the puzzle-piece island across from it labeled *Gladstone*. The map on the adjacent page was of Gladstone alone. It showed a ferry landing facing directly across from Destiny Falls' ferry landing. There was topography that showed lakes, rivers, and mountains, but not much else was called out on the map.

Neither Oliva nor Edna would discuss Gladstone. Why were they hiding something? Because here it was, big as life on the pages of this book, and it was located directly across from Destiny Falls. Certainly, they would know more about the island and why it was forbidden to travel there.

I poured myself a fresh cup of cookie-free tea and settled in to read through the book.

Chapter One started with another map. This one showed the crescent-shaped island of Destiny Falls and the opposite-shaped island of Gladstone pushed together to form one larger island. It was labeled in the corner: *United States Naval Observatory, Circa 1800*.

That seemed very odd. I Googled *How many years does it take for an island to divide?* That brought no matches, so I changed the word from *island* to *continent*. There were more matches, and I couldn't find an exact answer, except that it seemed to take millions of years for the movement of tectonic plates that could separate a land mass.

The book somewhat answered my question in the next section, when it referred to '*The Great Divide*':

It has always been assumed that Destiny Falls and Gladstone were at one time joined as one larger island because of the precisely matching coastlines. A Naval Observatory map discovered in the early 1900s appeared to confirm this. The map showed a date stamp of 'Circa 1800,' but it was unclear if the map was found then or created at that time. There was no background information to clarify when The Great Divide of the two islands occurred.

The last chapter was labeled *The Myths*. Here's where it got really interesting.

Over the years, many myths have surrounded the island of Gladstone. Most often, they have to do with magical lakes, though what magic they have isn't always clear. The most intriguing myth is one of a lake that functions much like a fountain of youth, providing a person with the power to remain ageless.

The island is protected in ways that prevent travelers from reaching it, though many try. It is rumored that some of those who try actually do reach the island. However, once they arrive, they find a normal town that functions like any port community.

The town of Gladstone is said to be surrounded by forested lands and mountains. Additional myths exist that tell of adventurers who are lost in the mountains while searching for the magical lakes.

Those who have traveled successfully to Gladstone and returned home hoard their secrets about what they'd seen and experienced. It's rumored that danger befalls those who tell of it.

I knew about the concept of magical lakes after my experience at Twin Falls Lake, so the myth could easily be based on reality. Well, the distorted reality of this place. The fountain of youth would explain why people would want to travel there, even though terrible things could happen, according to Olivia, and now this book as well.

This book was frustratingly short and assumed the reader knew the basic history of the islands and the myths already. I would need to visit the historical book room again. Ahh! First, I'd go to the *Observer* office. I could look through more old papers. Perhaps I could locate a directory of past issues or topics to see if Gladstone was mentioned. Maybe I could find something that expanded on the details of Gladstone, the myths, and the Great Divide.

I was feeling tired from spending the morning sorting files on the floor and then sitting here studying the book. I decided that a short yoga session would revive me, then I'd head to the *Observer*. It felt rude to leave my teacup and cookie mess here for someone else to clean up, but the magical tea cart fairy seemed to always have that covered.

I changed into yoga pants and a tee, grabbed a towel, and went into my yoga room. As always, I glanced in the oval mirror as I passed. A tingle of joy zapped through my body as I saw that I was looking into Luna's apartment! It appeared I was looking through the makeup mirror on her bedroom dresser. She had her back to me and was holding a watering can. She watered the plants and left the room, likely to water the other plants throughout the house.

There was no way was I going to just stand here and watch her walk away again! I zipped out to my bedroom and grabbed my cell phone and sent her a text. I hoped she would get it.

LUNA!!!!!

HAYDEN!!!!

LOL

I typed a note to her and then hoped with all my heart that the DF Satellite would not block it, as it had before. I had to be careful. I did not want to be responsible for Luna being sucked into Destiny Falls and forced to leave her entire family behind.

Don't freak out. I will explain.
Follow these directions exactly.

Huh? What are you talking about?!

Go look in the makeup mirror on your dresser.
If the room looks wavy or you see a flash of light,
immediately hit the floor and crawl out of the
room.
I know that sounds weird. You have to trust me.

Is this like a riddle or something?
I don't get it.

No! Not a riddle. Go look in the mirror
—but get out of there if things look wavy
or there's a bright light.

Seriously Hayden. You're scaring me.
Have you been abducted by aliens?

No aliens! But it's very strange.
Don't freak out. I'll explain.

Yeah. You already said that.

Are you going?

Ooookay. I'm going.

I stared into the mirror as if I could make my friend appear by sheer willpower. A minute later, she entered the bedroom. I saw her creeping up to the mirror like she expected it to pop like a jack-in-the-box. She stepped up close and I gave her my biggest smile and waved with both arms.

I could hear no sound, but it was clear that Luna was screaming. She turned around and ran out of the bedroom. I dialed her, but the call failed. I texted her, but got not no reply.

I sat at my computer and composed a note to explain to Luna what she was seeing. I rewrote it three times to get it just right. I finally hit send.

Undeliverable: Message has failed to be delivered to this recipient.

I slumped over and banged my head on the desk. Argh! Had her frightened response severed our connection? Could I get it back? I would try every day until I made it happen. And I absolutely would not give up until I made it happen.

20

The Witch

The witch braided and twisted her long blond hair into the *I Dream of Jeannie* hairdo and plunked the ridiculous red and pink cap on top of her head. She loved having such thick, youthful hair again, but she missed her wash-and-wear style. She hadn't been creating this updo lately, opting instead for an easy ponytail. But today was special. Today she had guests coming. She applied a slick of pink lipstick and glued on the stupid long eyelashes. She tidied up her bottle-inspired décor and fluffed the many pointless throw pillows. At last, she was ready.

The witch sat near her doorway and listened. She could hear the three bumbling men making their way up the mountain. Oh, fiddle-sticks. By the sound of their grunting and arguing, it appeared she'd hired another batch of nincompoops. Well, even nincompoops could get a job done if they had the right management, and it seems she may have gotten that part correct, since they'd already completed part one. It was time to meet these clowns in person and send a message to their bosses to put part two into play. Such clandestine nonsense. But necessary to cover their tracks.

She tapped her foot and clicked her pink nails on the arm of the wooden rocker. They were taking their sweet old time getting up here.

Finally, she heard a ruckus at the entrance to her cave. "About dang time," she muttered.

The witch got her first look at the three men from her Ring doorbell video camera. She checked them out as they walked up to the cave and rang the bell.

"Who dares to approach my doorway? "she bellowed in her ominous witch voice. Then she covered her mouth and snickered as they all jumped back and hovered together.

"We are the representatives for Lazarus and the Commander," one guy answered.

"Enter!" she roared as she pushed the button that caused the door to groan open. Cripes, she missed having her full powers. Having to push a button and watch a video screen was so, so, ummm, Human! She cringed at the word.

The three men walked in through the oversized wooden door and entered the cave. Their jaws dropped and they were shocked speechless. The inside of the cave was a replica of Jeannie's magic bottle, and the woman standing before them looked like Jeannie herself, harem costume, blond updo, and all.

They were standing there staring at her, so she crossed her arms, nodded her head, and blinked. A light flurry of snowflakes came down on their heads. Oh, it would cost her a bit of magic, but the looks on their faces made it all worth it.

In an instant, her mood soured. "Enough play time," she roared in her witchy voice, batting away a few flakes that drifted her way. "Have you brought the items from my list?"

One man spoke up. "You can make it snow, but you can't get your own groceries?"

His companion whispered, "Be quiet," but not soon enough.

The witch glared at him and pointed an oddly boney finger for such a young woman. "You know nothing of my magic and how it works!" He coughed, and his partners backed away as his tongue grew five times its size.

She would never say it out loud, but she had no idea how her magic worked now either. Since she'd been banished to this dreadful cave, her magic was frustratingly limited and inconsistent. If she could get these idiots to do her bidding, she might finally get out of this prison and on with her life.

"The list!" she roared.

The men put their bags in front of her, including the one whose tongue had shrunk back to normal size, but who was now wise enough to stay quiet.

The Jeannie-ized witch came forward and unpacked the bags, nodding her approval. The men watched as she gleefully sorted through mundane groceries. Ramen noodles, Keebler cookies, a six-pack of light beer, a huge brick of cheddar cheese, several boxes of crackers, and a super-sized bag of gummy worms.

She stepped over her loot and stood in front of them.

"Well done on taking care of the boat lady." She nodded at them. She had learned that compliments would keep people on track. She was clumsy at it, but it still seemed to work. They looked proud. Ridiculous men.

"Have Lazarus and the Commander taken control of the operation?"

The three looked at each other, but no one spoke.

"Do. Not. Make. Me. Repeat. Myself." She loved to use that angry mother's voice. It always worked.

"Not yet," said the same guy as before. "But the transfer of power is in process. The investigation into the captain's death is still ongoing. We've planted the rumor about her affair, and we bribed her estranged husband into staying hidden in Gladstone. The next step is to . . ."

"Stop!" The witch put her hand to her ear. "Someone is outside listening." She tilted her head to concentrate.

"You fools!" she screeched. "How did you let someone follow you here?"

She flipped on her Ring doorbell camera screen. A hiker was standing right outside the door, listening.

"Go!" She pointed to the door as she pressed the button to open it.

An Asian man in full hiking gear was standing beside her cave. He was obviously eavesdropping. Too bad he was so handsome. It was a shame to dispose of him.

"Get rid of the witness!" she thundered in her most menacing voice.

The men scrambled to do her bidding.

21

Three men were loitering in front of the *Observer* office when I arrived. One guy was sitting on the bench, the other two standing nearby. They all turned to look at me when I walked up to my door.

"Morning, ma'am," said the one on the bench.

For the record, I really hated when people called me ma'am. In my opinion, that should be reserved for senior citizens. I mean *really* senior, like centenarians. I'd even prefer a *hey, you* over a *ma'am*. Ugh. Still, it was meant to be polite, so I smiled and said hello.

The other two men answered in turn. One of them was tall and thin. He was wearing a bow tie, black glasses, and a handlebar mustache. He smiled, showing off his gold tooth. Then he winked and gave me a salute. He wasn't a person I could easily forget. It was the same man I had seen in Vessie's café.

Then the original guy spoke up. "Are you Hayden, then?"

"Yes, I am." I held my keys up as if proof of my identity. "The new editor of the *Observer*." I felt myself blush when I said that, like I was an imposter. But it was true! This was part of my new identity.

"Welcome to the business district," said mustache man. "I'm Lester. Pharmacist." He pointed to the pharmacy across the street. He reached out, and we shook hands.

"Vito," said a heavyset man wearing overalls. "Mine's the hardware store just down the block. And this here's Archibald." He gestured to the third man.

"It's my shop next door," said Archibald, the man sitting on the bench. "Time Travels On. Antiques."

I leaned over and shook his hand. "That's an interesting store name."

"Was my wife's idea. She's gone now, but I kept the shop name."

"Oh, I'm sorry for your loss," I said.

Archibald laughed. Then all three men snickered, and Vito spoke up. "She ain't dead, just gone outta his life. Good riddance to her. She's a menace." The other two nodded.

"So, you're reviving the old paper, huh?" Vito asked me, thankfully changing the subject.

"I am. Though it will be online now, instead of print."

He nodded. "Makes sense. Bring us into the twentieth century."

"Uh," Archibald interrupted, "you mean the twenty-first century, buddy."

"Yeah, yeah, whatever," said Vito, waving away the comment. "Modern times, modern paper." He squinted his eyes at me. "You gonna start being all nosy and poking into everyone's business now?"

"Dang, Vito!" said Lester, the pharmacist. "That's rude, man."

I was feeling prematurely grateful for his defense when he finished his thought.

"Poking into people's business *is* the editor's job." He snorted, as if proud of his joke. They all started snickering again.

"So, girly," said Vito. "When's the first issue of this here online paper?"

I cringed at the 'girly,' but answered anyway. "I'm guessing it will take a month to get the first issue out. Lots to do in the meantime." I dropped a subtle hint that I needed to get to work. They totally missed it.

Archibald scratched his bald head—yeah, I thought it was funny that his name reflected his appearance—and spoke up. "You're lucky to snag the job. The newspaper's been closed up for near on a year."

"Has it been that long?" asked Lester, twisting his old-fashioned mustache like a villain in a black-and-white movie.

"Only 'bout six months," said Vito. "Cuz I remember it covered that break-in at the ferry office."

Lester looked annoyed and spoke up. "You mean the supposed break-in."

Ah, a clue? I'd have to go back to the old issues and look up the ferry office break-in. I wondered if it was related to the current case.

Vito sat down on the bench next to Archibald, crossed his legs, and laid his arm across the back of the seat. He looked like he was ready for a nice, long, comfortable visit. I was glad to meet fellow businesspeople, but I needed to eradicate myself from this chat fest so that I could start my research on the ferry captain and Gladstone.

"Livin' up at the Caldwell place now, right?" asked Archibald.

So much for removing myself from the conversation. I opened my mouth to answer three seconds too late.

"Course she is!" said Vito. "She's a Caldwell. And them folks take care of their own. They're tight-knit, those Caldwells."

Lester laughed at that like it was some big joke. It didn't seem funny to me.

"Well, it's been great meeting you guys, I need to . . ."

Cut off at the knees by Lester. "Been up to Vessie's yet? It's just around the corner and she makes a mean Reuben sandwich."

"I could go for a Reuben," said Vito.

"Don't think she serves lunch stuff this early," Archibald said.

"I could for an omelet, then."

The three stood up.

"You comin'?" Vito looked at me expectantly.

"Thank you for the invite, but I have a lot

of work to do. Better get to it!" I smiled brightly to take the sting out of turning down their invitation.

"Next time, then. Good day, ma'am," said Archibald, tipping an imaginary hat. Then the three of them ambled down the sidewalk toward Vessie's Café.

The newspaper office embraced me with its quiet, library-like ambiance. I felt comfortable here, perhaps because of my love of libraries mixed with my journalism background. I stowed my purse and keys under the front counter and took stock of the office.

Before I started digging through the previous issues, I thought I'd look for a directory or list of topics covered. I booted up the computer and typed in the password that my father had provided: ObservPaperPW1. If they needed other passwords, I'd bet they'd be the same, but ending in PW2 or PW3.

The desktop files were pretty much what I'd expect in a newspaper office. Everything was divided up into four major categories: editorial, production, circulation, and advertising. I opened the editorial section and scanned the file names. I found one named *Headlines*. A good place to start.

I opened the file and found that the headlines were grouped by year, so I opened the most recent year. I grabbed a notepad and made a list of topics to search:

Ferry Captain / Nakita Morozova, Destiny Falls Ferry, Gladstone, Ferry break-in / Local break-in, The Great Divide

I searched each topic and wrote down the dates of any matches. I ended up with quite a few. Nothing on Gladstone or The Great Divide, though. I shut down the computer and started my search of the newspaper drawers, pulling out issues that matched my topic dates.

My focus was so intense that I didn't even hear someone come in until the front door clicked shut behind him. Startled, I looked up to see my father standing near the counter. I decided my next purchase would be a bell for the doorknob. I wondered if the hardware store had them.

"Thought I might find you here," he said. "How's it going?"

"Great! The previous editor was very organized. Makes it easier to find my way around."

"That's good." He nodded at my stack of newspapers. "Planning on some light reading?"

"The best way to get familiar with the newspaper, right?"

He nodded in agreement. "Any questions I can help with?" he asked.

"I'm just getting into things, but I'm sure I'll have plenty. I'm wondering when I'm expected to have the first issue out?"

My father explained that there was no actual deadline, and they trusted I'd know how to put things together since I already ran an on-line magazine. He said that everyone was happy to know that the paper would be up and running again. He felt that a small town benefited from the cohesiveness of a local paper. Word on the street was that people were excited about it. That was good—a paper needed advertising, so I hoped the community businesses would be up for buying ads.

"Want some help?" my father asked. "I have the rest of the day open."

"I'd love that, thank you!" I slid the paper with my topic list under my stack since I wasn't ready to divulge any information about the box, fearing the warning of danger to my family. I asked if he'd mind checking the computer and helping me put together a list of businesses who might purchase advertising. After all, that was usually the first order of business for a small periodical. No ads—no paper.

"Would you like some tea?" I asked.

He nodded. "Um-hmm." Just like me, he was quick to get to work. He was already reading something on the screen. I made us both a cup of tea in the small convenience kitchen, then sat on the floor in front of the newspaper drawers.

My father sat at the desk and was clicking away at the computer, while I continued to look through the past issues. We enjoyed small talk and some companionable silence. A few hours passed while we worked. It was nice to be connecting with my father like this. Working together seemed to bring us closer.

We took a break for dinner, grabbing take-out from the deli just a block away and eating in the small park. We talked about the paper, and he also offered more tips about working with my camera. In a new relationship, it always helps to have a common interest, and I felt this could be it.

The conversation turned away from work and we talked about life in general.

"You seem to be settling in nicely here. Like you fit right in. Not just to the family, but with the town too."

"That's true," I said. "It feels like home here. There's just something about it, almost like it was always here for me, waiting."

"Well, I for one kept your place open," He paused and touched his heart. "I hoped one day you'd be here. Not to be entirely selfish, but now that I have you here, I'll do everything I can to keep you!" He paused and chuckled. "Well, that sounded sinister! I didn't mean it that way!"

"Bwah-haha!" I laughed in a villainous voice. That got him laughing even more.

When we finally stopped laughing, he spoke up. "I was thinking, Hayden. I'd love it if you called me Dad. Father is way too formal for me, and I think Leonard makes it sound like I'm the guy next door." He chuckled. "That is if you'd be comfortable with it?"

At that moment, I felt it. An emotion that was different from any other in my life. A father-daughter bond that was growing and solidifying. And yes. It felt right.

"I'd love that," I said. ". . .Dad."

He got up from the bench and put his arm around me for a fatherly hug. I felt we'd pivoted in our relationship, and now, for the first time in my life, I had a Dad.

We finished up our meal and took a leisurely stroll down the street. It was just getting dark and the streetlights were coming on. Businesses were lit up from inside, looking warm and cozy as we passed. The whole downtown had a soft, almost holiday-like glow to it.

We headed back to the office, and my dad offered to stay and finish up the work we'd started. Yeah, my dad. How cool was that?

"You sure it's not too late?" I asked.

"Nah. I'm good. Could use some tea though."

This made me wonder if I had inherited my dedicated work ethic—and my love of tea—from him. I could go for hours when I was focused on a project. I made us both tea and brought it back to the desk.

He located the information on the previous advertisers. I noticed that the hardware store, the antique shop, and the pharmacy were all listed.

"I met three of the local business owners this morning," I told him.

"Really? Who'd you meet?"

I told him about Archibald, Lester, and Vito. He laughed. "Well, you couldn't have picked a more unusual trio to start with."

"Yeah. They're quite the characters," I agreed. "They seemed interested and supportive of the paper, though. I feel like I can approach them about ads."

"There you go! Your first set of contacts. That's my girl!"

I felt a rush of pride when he said that. I had always had plenty of praise from Nana and Gran, yet having him compliment me was a whole new kind of joy.

Both of our phones pinged text messages at the same time. I glanced at my screen and saw a message from Axel.

Han in hiking accident.
Just got him to the hospital.

My father's face drained of color and registered the shock and panic that I was feeling. He had received the same message. I grabbed my purse and keys, locked the door, and we drove to the hospital.

We arrived at the hospital to find Eleanor, Phillip, and Axel in the waiting area. Axel was pacing the room anxiously.

I reached out and gently touched Axel's arm. "How's Han doing? What happened?"

"He went hiking up to Twin Falls Lake early this morning. He always leaves his hiking itinerary with one of his sisters. When he didn't return on time, she gave Jaxson a call. Han is experienced. He's quick and responsible. When he didn't text or call, we knew something wasn't right."

"Jax and I booked it up to the lake. We found him unconscious at the base of a cliff. Jax called in the park's rescue helicopter, and they brought us in. Han is still unconscious, but stable."

"Can we see him?" I asked.

"Family only right now. His sisters are in there with him. We were just waiting for an update from the doctors."

Tears filled my eyes, and I felt my throat tighten. I could barely swallow, and I couldn't speak. I hoped with everything in me that Han would be okay.

22

My first thought upon waking was of Han. It hit me hard. I put my hand to my stomach and waited for the nausea to pass and my breathing to return to normal. The soft, warm feeling of the cat huddle lying close to my back was soothing. I willed my body to relax.

When we'd left the hospital last night, Han had still been unconscious. The doctor told us it was normal to lose consciousness for six hours or more after a traumatic head injury, so I hoped there was good news this morning. Was it too early to text Axel for an update? I hoped not, but I needed to know. I reached over the sleeping cat heap and snatched my phone.

Good morning Axel.
I hope I didn't wake you.
Any news about Han?

Morning Sis! No worries. I was up.
Han regained consciousness in the
middle of the night. He's woozy and
can't recall what happened. But the
doctor says he looks good.

Oh! Thank God! I've

been so worried.

> *Me, too. I'm going to stop by*
> *and see him later. Want to come?*

Yes, please!

> *Leaving at 10:00. Afterwards meeting up*
> *with Jax for lunch at Vessie's. Sound good?*

Sounds wonderful! See you at 10.

I slipped out of bed and got dressed, then peeked into the yoga room mirror. The depressing reflection was of the yoga room. The disappointment left a heaviness in my heart. I sent Luna a brief text.

> *Hey, friend. I hope you're okay.*
> *I know you were pretty shocked.*
> *It's a weird situation. Text or*
> *email when you can. Would*
> *love to explain what you saw.*

I held my breath and stared at the screen, hoping the satellite would allow it to pass. The text was sent! Now I hoped Luna would read it and reply. I sat down on a yoga mat and waited, but there was no immediate response. I'd let her settle with this for a while, and if she didn't answer, I'd try her again tomorrow.

I opened my photos and tapped on the folder connected to my *Observer* camera. I got a lump in my throat looking at the pictures of the owl that Han helped me with. I enjoyed that time with him so much. It was spooky to think that the next time he went hiking there he would have a terrible fall. It would be good to see him today with my own eyes.

I scrolled back in the photos and came across the ones I had taken on my first day with the camera. The day that the mail carrier had been assaulted. I barely remembered snapping these pictures. I'd been so upset seeing him lying on the ground.

I looked more closely at the photos now. In one picture I noticed a spot of bright red in the middle of all the landscaping. The flowers that day were in shades of blue, yellow, and white. There were no red flowers anywhere else in the picture. Just that one bright red spot.

I enlarged the photo. The red was not flowers. It was hair! It was the head of a short, heavy person, and he was walking around to the side of the house. Actually, since he was slightly blurry compared to the rest of the picture, it was more like he was running. I enlarged further and saw the backside of a second person in the photo, just in front of him. And that person was very tall, extremely large, and appeared to be wearing a greasy-looking ferry uniform.

I pressed my fingers over my mouth to cover my gasp and tried to control my panic. This meant that Kerbie and one of the mechanics were at Caldwell Crest that day. From the back they looked the same, so I couldn't tell who this was. Or was the other mechanic there also, out of camera range? What reason would they have to be there? Did they attack the mail carrier and dig through the mail? Were they looking for the box that arrived later that day?

I had been keeping it secret because of the captain's warning of danger to me and my family. Were these men the danger? I dropped my phone on the mat and tried hard to corral my wild thoughts. Now what? I couldn't keep hiding these secrets, could I? Should I? Perhaps this was evidence of the attackers from that day. Were they also the ones responsible for the captain's death?

Now I was just working myself up into a frenzy. I needed to focus my thoughts and make the right decisions.

The box. Perhaps it held more clues to what was going on. I grabbed my phone and sent the photos to my e-mail to make sure I had a backup copy. Then I sent a second copy to my *Natural Living* e-mail, just to be sure. Perhaps I should share the photos with Jaxson today? The photos weren't part of the box. I could ask him to keep it in confidence. If he knew, but told no one else, would that lead to danger . . . or to an arrest?

I dragged the box out of the closet and placed it in the middle of my bedroom floor. It seemed critical now to get a handle on what was in those files. If this box was what they were after, there must be something of great importance in here. But what exactly? Now that I'd learned more about Gladstone, I suspected it had to do with that forbidden island, the magical lakes, and the fountain of youth.

Time to get serious. I had a couple of hours before meeting up with Axel. I would spend the time searching through the files. I took a deep breath and slapped my hands on the top of the box, then cringed at the loud bang. No need to wake the cats!

"Yowzer! What was that?" Latifa asked.

Oops. Too late. Cat number one was up.

"Sorry, Latifa. I didn't mean to wake you," I whispered.

"If you didn't mean to wake me, you shouldn't be playing bongo drums on that box."

"Go back to sleep." I used a kind voice to take the edge off my words. "I have work to do."

"Too late, Honey Pie. I'm up now." I heard her moving around on the bed. *"Aww. Look at this cutie patootie sound asleep. Isn't she precious?"*

"Um, hmm." I was already removing files from the box.

"Hayden! I said look at the cutie patootie!"

To keep her quiet, I stood up and looked at

the bed. "Ah, yes. She's the sweetest little thing."

"And look at Chanel. She's like a sleeping angel."

I sat back down until I heard Latifa clear her throat. That meant a reply was necessary. I stood back up and looked at Chanel curled up on the bed. Her pristine, white fur a contrast to Lola's rich, black fuzz. "My, she's such a pretty cat. You can feel the softness of her fur without even touching it."

Appeased, Latifa lay back down, yawned, and closed her eyes.

The brief exchange with my cat helped to calm my spirit. I felt a touch more back on earth. I pulled more files out of the box. I opened the two folders with the payment ledgers. Then noticed there were two more just like them. There had to be fifty pages of names altogether. The lack of dates was odd.

The large dollar amounts had me thinking. These were not normal boat fares, not that anything in Destiny Falls was normal, but the prices in stores and restaurants here seemed typical. Using that as a gauge, these were excessively high. I'd traveled on many ferry boats back in Seattle, and even the most expensive trips were just a fraction of these amounts. The cruise ship idea popped back in my head, but it made no sense. Perhaps this all had to do with the island of Gladstone. People would pay sizeable sums to achieve the fountain of youth. Many would risk dangerous situations to find it.

I noticed that they often wrote one column in different color ink, so it was likely filled in at a different time. It was the column that showed either *Approved* or *Denied*. Why would one need approval for a journey? And who did the approving or denying?

Then there was the column for *Agent*—either A, K, or V. And finally *Paid*—to either L or M. And every person showed paid, whether approved or not.

I scanned the pages of names. Mostly, the names were common enough. There were a few that sounded foreign, but not an excessive amount of those. The names were handwritten, printed first, and then a signature as if the people themselves had signed in on the page. Interestingly, I noticed that a few names were listed more than once—sometimes just a few pages apart, other times in an entirely different folder. I was speeding through the pages now, not seeing anything unusual, until my eye caught the name Caldwell.

I rubbed my eyes, then leaned closer to the page to decipher the curvy handwriting. As the name became clear to me, the hair on the back of my neck stood up and my throat went dry.

Shock and confusion washed over me. I could hear my own heartbeat pounding in my ears. I sucked in a breath and bolted upright. The file dropped off my lap onto the floor. It lay there, looking like a normal file, filled with normal papers. But I knew that it wasn't. I reached out to the desk for support and stared down at the papers. There was nothing normal about this at all. Clear as day, the name on the page was Emily Caldwell . . . *Denied.*

23

Why was my mother's name on this page? I ran my finger over the curvy, bold signature. Was this really her? Did she sign this page? Was she trying to leave Destiny Falls or trying to come here? She had been denied. There was no date. Was this recent or from years ago? Was this one of the secrets that the ferry captain was warning me about? Was my mother in danger? Or . . . was *she* the danger?

Emotions traveled through my body in waves. My mother who disappeared when I was two days old. My mother who never explained why she left or where she went. Was she somehow tied to the mystery of the ferry?

My father's life originated in Destiny Falls, and he had escaped from here to Seattle as a young man, where he met and married my mother. They had a wonderful life together. They lived with my Nana and Gran. They had Axel and me. Then he disappeared without a trace on the day of my birth, not to be heard from again. I now knew that was when he and Axel were captured and transported to Destiny Falls, where they were trapped, unable to return to us.

My mother had disappeared two days later. We had always assumed that because she was a young mother with a new baby, suddenly without a husband, that she was overwhelmed with panic and fled. Perhaps we didn't know the truth? Was there a similar mystery to the disappearance of Emily, my mother?

Inexplicably, I started to laugh, then it turned into crying. Then I was laughing and crying at the same time. Could people even do that? Apparently, they could. For a while, I rode my roller-coaster of emotions without even trying to control them.

Finally, I lay on the floor and did a series of movements that I often use when I want to relieve stress, and oh, did I feel stress right now. I ended up with the corpse pose—worst name ever for a yoga position—and lay flat on my back, my arms spread out at my sides. Instead of closing my eyes, though, I looked up at the ceiling, my mind spinning with possibilities and questions.

I finally sat up with renewed energy and snapped a photo of the section of the page where my mother's name was written. Then I took a photo of the entire page, plus the ones before and after it. I'd look up some of the names at the newspaper office or maybe the library. Perhaps it would lead to a clue about when these pages had been created or information about the people listed. I packed up the box and stored it back in my closet.

While dressing to meet Axel, I made the decision that at lunch I would show him and Jaxson the photos of the mail carrier's attack scene and point out what I'd discovered. I also decided not to share anything about the box or finding our mother's name on the ledger. It terrified me to think it might cause dangerous repercussions, based on Nakita's warning, and the very real occurrence of her death. What if I opened a literal Pandora's Box and allowed danger into our family? I couldn't risk that.

Axel led the conversation on our drive to the hospital with an update on Han's condition. "Han can't remember the accident. He has no idea what happened. The doctor said it's common to be unable to recall events immediately before, during, and after a head trauma event. All that Han remembers is being on a hike up to the lake. He's very frustrated because he's done that trail many times, and he's an experienced hiker and climber. He doesn't know why he'd put himself so close to a cliff edge, so he's angry at himself and confused."

"It's not his fault, I'm sure!" I instinctively jumped to Han's defense.

"The doctor said feeling responsible for the accident is normal. Also, that a patient's frustration with the inability to remember is normal. So, he suggested we don't ask him any questions about the accident right now."

"Okay, that makes sense. Does he have any other injuries?" I asked.

"A bump and gash on his head, which aligns with the concussion. He also has a broken arm and, of course, it would be his dominant arm. And apparently some cuts and scrapes consistent with a fall through the brush. He's an active guy, so being laid up and injured doesn't sit well with him. On top of that, he's dealing with another of the concussion symptoms—general mental fogginess and forgetfulness."

"I'm sure he's struggling with that," I said.

"Yeah, but the doctor says that trying to tough it out can make the concussion symptoms worse, so his sisters tried to convince him to stay with one of them for a few days. He was stubborn about that, so, apparently, they're going to take turns staying at his place. The doctor said his attitude is normal for a person suffering from these kinds of injuries, but that ignoring the symptoms can slow his recovery. So, he grudgingly agreed."

"Did the doctor say if he'll recover his memories of the accident?"

"It's possible. Though it could be weeks or even months. Some people never regain the memory of their accident. Only time will tell."

We pulled up to the hospital, and it impressed me to see a rather large, normal-looking city hospital, rather than more of a clinic, which is what I expected of a small town. Destiny Falls seemed to provide the best services for the people who lived here. The odd way that it moved parks and buildings around, the enchanted library, and the fact that it 'provided' Poppy's Extravaganza, I wondered if the town simply zapped the hospital in or if humans built it in the usual way.

We checked in at the front desk and they gave us directions to Han's room. We walked in to see him standing in front of the closet, gathering his belongings, apparently ready to hightail it out of there.

"Hey, dude," said Axel. "Did the doctor give you the okay to be up and about like this?"

"Hello to you too," said Han, clumsily shoving his clothes into a backpack with his left hand, his right in a cast and sling. Then he saw me, and his face lit up with a brilliant smile. "Hayden!"

"Hi. How're you feeling?"

"Well, now that you're here, I'm 100 percent better."

"Woah," said Axel, "What about me? Doesn't my presence rate?"

"Not when you come charging in like one of my sisters. I've had quite enough nagging from them, thank you very much. I don't need any more from you." But he softened his words by giving Axel a smile and a playful punch to the arm. After which Axel moaned and held his supposedly injured shoulder.

"They're granting my freedom later today. I'm waiting to clear the paperwork with the doctor. Yanay and Eva are on the way here to drive me home. They feel like they need to babysit me for a few days, and the doctor is fueling their motherly instincts."

"Well, if your mother was still here, she'd be doing the same," said Axel. "Let them take care of you, Han. It's good for them."

"But it will be the death of me!" laughed Han.

Every time someone mentioned *death* these days, even in jest, it made me shiver. I was a little hypersensitive since the captain's unsolved murder, not to mention dealing with the murder case from a month ago. That was exactly two more murders than I'd ever dealt with in my life.

We convinced Han to climb back into the bed while we packed up the rest of his belongings for him. He started to look tired, so Axel suggested a nap. Han first complained about being treated like a kindergartener, but Axel reminded him that the doctor had said that he would need much more sleep than normal during this recovery. Finally, he succumbed to the tiredness. We left, entrusting his care to the capable hospital staff and his two sisters, who were on the way.

As we left his room, we passed a volunteer pushing a flower cart, delivering flowers and balloons to all the patients on the floor. She waved cheerily as she passed us. I did a double-take and knew in an instant who the volunteer was. Not too many hospital volunteers looked like this. She was a tall woman, wearing a white mini-dress with a flowing pink cape. She rocked white, knee-high socks and pink, patent leather stilettos. She had a white-blond ponytail cascading down under a red cap festooned with sparkles. Yep, Cleobella volunteered at the hospital.

When Axel and I arrived at Vessie's, Jaxson was already seated at a booth. Vessie was standing beside it chatting with him. They both looked up and waved as we came in.

The café today looked pretty much the same as the last time I was here, which in Destiny Falls was quite a surprise. I had come to expect the subtle—and sometimes not so subtle—changes in the buildings around here. It's like they had a mind of their own. I didn't blame the café for remaining the same. It was charming and cheerful, exactly as it was, in all its beautiful, pink glory.

Vessie gifted me her usual warm hug and kind welcome, and she did the same for Axel. She took our drink orders—tea for me, of course—and went off to the kitchen, while we settled in with Jaxson. Axel slid into the booth, sat across from Jaxson, and plunked himself right in the middle, while Jax scooted over to make room for me on his side. He put his arm around me for a quick, friendly hug. I found that Jaxson was feeling more like a brother to me—or more accurately, a brother's best friend—than a potential date. That was really for the best, though. If we dated and it didn't work out, it might forever be uncomfortable between us. And I enjoyed being with these two far too much to jeopardize the friendship.

We scanned our menus, and all agreed that the special of the day was the winner. Quarter-pound bacon and avocado burgers with fries and a milkshake. Luckily, I was taking a hike with Olivia after our lunch, so I could work off the extra calories. Knowing what great food Vessie served here, it would be well worth it.

While we waited for our food, Jaxson gave us an update on the case of the ferry captain's murder.

"We were certain this was a crime of passion tied to the captain's contentious divorce and affair, but we've hit several roadblocks. We've been unable to unearth the name of the man involved in the supposed affair; all we've heard so far is hearsay. The captain's husband is apparently out of town and unreachable. We've yet to be able to contact him to notify him of the death. His timely disappearance raises questions, of course.

"We're looking for other family members or next of kin, but again, finding nothing. We've done a complete search of the victim's home and office and came up empty. There is little information under the name Nakita Morozova, so that leads us to believe it was an alias, or perhaps her maiden name, but not her legal name. At first glance, this was a simple case, but it's gotten complicated. The investigation is still underway."

"Wow, that's crazy," said Axel. "You never know what people are hiding under their nondescript, everyday exteriors."

That seemed to be my opening, so I dove right in. "Speaking of hidden things, I have something to show you."

Both men looked my way and gave me their full attention. It made me squirm.

"The day that the mail carrier was attacked at Caldwell Crest was the first day I had my *Observer* work camera. I had it with me at that moment and snapped a few pictures at the scene. In the panic of the situation, I had forgotten I took the shots. I was looking at them this morning and noticed something odd."

I pulled out my phone and clicked on the photo I had copied and saved in a separate file.

"Look right here. I realized that there were no red flowers in the yard, but there was one bright splash of red." I turned the phone their way. Then I opened the next photo, which was an enlarged section of the first, and pointed at the red-haired person in the bushes.

"That's definitely Kerbie, the helmsman. He's unmistakable," said Jaxson. "And is that one of the ferry mechanics? Gronk or Shrek? Why were they at Caldwell Crest?"

"There'd be no reason that I know of," said Axel.

As they were looking at the pictures, I reminded them of another fact. "Remember that even though they were known to be friends, Nakita appeared nervous around the mechanics the first day that I met her. And the two of them, plus Kerbie, were at the scene when they removed her body from the ferry that day."

"That's a few too many coincidences. Hayden, can you forward that photo to me, please?" asked Jaxson. "We'll look into it. Thanks for lunch, guys. I'm going to get this info over to the station."

Jaxson hustled out of the café. We finished up and said our goodbyes to Vessie. Axel offered to drop me off at Olivia's for our hike through the park. I was looking forward to it. Perhaps Olivia would share new gossip and spill a few more secrets today. Maybe I could prod her into telling me what she knew about my mother, because I was sure she knew something.

24

With all the madness around me lately, I'd gotten away from my usual jogging and hiking routine. I was feeling anxious about it since I did not want to slip back into my old patterns of exercise avoidance. I was grateful that Olivia was a hiker, and since she was retired, she was always up for a hike. In addition, she was chatty as she walked, and today that might come in handy.

The day, as always, was perfect. A bright blue sky held a smattering of perfectly spaced, white clouds lit by bright sunshine. Hmm. How did Destiny Falls control its own weather? That seemed like high-level magic to me. And it must rain sometime to maintain all the gorgeous vegetation. Maybe it rained in the night while I slept and brought out the sun with the morning? Another question about this peculiar place.

Olivia, Hercules, and I were slowly making our way down the path at the entry to the park. In this area, the path was wide enough for the three of us. It was made of woodchips and gravel, so the level surface enabled us to focus on our conversation instead of our feet.

I told Olivia about my visit with Han and gave her an update on his condition.

"It surprised me to hear that Han had a hiking accident," Olivia said. "With his background, you would think he'd be pretty much indestructible!"

"What background do you mean?" I asked.

She stumbled around her sentence. "Well, umm, I just mean, umm, he's done so much hiking here, he should have the routes memorized by now."

I gave her the side-eye. "What aren't you telling me, Olivia?"

"Oh. Well. That's not for me to tell," she said. "If you get to know Han well enough, he might share some of his background. But it's not for me to say."

She'd already started to say, but there was no point in pushing her. I really loved Olivia, but she had a way of slipping just bits of information into a conversation and then backpedaling when she realized she had said too much, which was not unusual. Once she clammed up, that would be it. I changed the subject.

"I heard something weird about Nakita's case today. Apparently, they haven't been able to learn the name of the man she was having an affair with."

"Affair?!" Olivia stared at me in shock. "Is that what they're saying?"

"Yes, they're thinking it may have been a crime of passion, because of the affair and her contentious divorce."

"That is absolutely absurd," Olivia said. "I happen to know that Nakita and her husband have been separated for over a year. They both are dating other people. Affair, my foot!"

"They also said her husband is out of town and they can't locate him."

"Well, of course he is! He moved away from Destiny Falls after they separated. I heard he got special approval to move to Glad . . . um, to move away."

"Were you going to say Gladstone?"

Suddenly she became quite interested in what Hercules was looking at—just a bird.

"Olivia? No one wants to talk about Gladstone. Why is that?"

"Hayden, there are some topics that are off-limits for good reason, and this is one of those. It's got a long, complicated, and sinister history that is partially concealed. It's forbidden to travel there unless you gain special approval—which is extremely difficult to get."

Wow. Olivia had never spoken to me that way and she'd never been so outright secretive about something being the queen of gossip. It elevated my concerns about the warnings I'd received and the mystery box as well.

"How do you even apply for such an approval to travel there?"

"That's part of the secrecy that surrounds the islands. People don't even know how it's done until one day they do."

"Don't people ever travel there on their own, without permission?" I asked.

"If you do, you'll likely just arrive to find yourself right back at home. We honestly don't even know what we don't know. I would strongly suggest you drop the subject and stop asking about it."

I thought about how that statement kind of summed up Destiny Falls. I didn't know what I didn't know. I just kept finding out more things a bit at a time.

We walked in silence for a while. She seemed very focused on her dog and the view, but I knew she hoped that I would stop asking questions about Gladstone. I would. For now. But I'd continue to research this odd story.

As long as I was trying to pry information from her, it was time to see if I could gain any intel on my mother.

"I know you've lived here your entire life, and you've known my father and Axel since he was a toddler. Did you know anything about my mother?"

I was watching Olivia when I asked her this question, and I could see the blush creep up her face and her eyes darting around. Her voice came out just an octave too high. "Your mother?"

"Yes, my mother."

"Well, she's never been to Destiny Falls, so no, I've never met her."

"But do you know of her?"

"Maybe. I've heard some things."

"Olivia, please!" I stopped walking, faced her, and touched her arm. "I've never been told anything about her. I would really like to know something. Anything."

"Let's just say . . . that I've heard that she's a lovely woman and that she never got over losing your father."

"Have you ever heard about where she lives —or lived?" I asked.

Olivia started biting her thumbnail and reached down to pet Hercules with fast, jerky movements. "You can never tell anyone that I told you this."

She paused and stared at me. "Hayden. You need to promise on your life. You won't tell anyone."

"Olivia, I promise. What do you know?"

She looked around to be sure we were alone, I suspected. Then she lowered her voice to a whisper and said, "I heard that she lived in Gladstone. But it was only a rumor. And that was many years ago."

25

The Witch

"What do you mean, 'He's not dead'!!!" the witch shrieked. For a split second the Jeannie-illusion was gone. She looked like a haggard, old crone. Then, in a flash, the pretty genie was back again.

The men backed against the wall and quivered.

"Why are you just telling me this now?" she yelled. "Well???"

One man spoke up. "We kinda just found out. But don't worry. I googled it. Many people with head injuries never remember the accident."

"You googled it? Oh, good."

The man totally missed her sarcasm and nodded his head. He looked relieved.

"You GOOGLED it?!" she screeched. Her eyes looked as if they were going to bulge right out of her head. "And this is supposed to make me feel better?" The old witch flickered again, and she looked angry. It was hard to see the anger when she looked like a perky, pink genie.

She paused a moment and counted slowly. "One . . . two . . . three . . . four . . . five."

The men stood silently and watched her.

She took a deep breath in through her nose

and let it out slowly through her mouth.

"Does Lazarus know this?" she asked.

"We didn't tell him. We thought we should tell you first."

"Good. Where is the spy now?" the Jeannie-witch asked in a calm voice.

Another man answered, "He's at home. Recovering."

"Is he alone?"

"No. He has two women there. And visitors in and out throughout every day."

"Then he has too many friends and people around him. That makes him a continued risk." She put her finger to her lip and tapped. "Keep an eye on him. Ask around. If there is any indication of his memory returning, I want to hear about it. Oh, a week later ought to do."

"Umm," said the man. "Why would we wait to tell you?"

"Oh, for Pete's sake!" she huffed. "It's sarcastic irony."

He stared at her blankly, so she continued.

"A linguistic device used to convey a meaning that is the opposite of its literal definition and intended to be caustic."

He continued to stand there silently gawking at her.

"Ack! Bunch of idiots! Go!!!" She pointed at the door. "Get out of my bottle and leave me in peace." She paused and appeared to gather her patience, then spoke in a pleasant voice. "Oh. Please pick up my grocery list from the table on your way out. Thank you for your business."

Then she crossed her arms, blinked, and nodded. Two giant bats flew down behind them, chasing the men out of the cave.

The witch snickered. "Whoopsie."

26

That evening, on my walk home from Olivia's, I called Jaxson with the additional information she had given me about the ferry captain. I told him Nakita had separated from her husband a year ago, they were both dating others, and that he had moved away back then. Jax was grateful for the new information. He said that if Olivia's facts were correct, it would eliminate the crime of passion angle. However, it set them back to square one on the case, as they had no other suspects or motives. They were going to investigate the possible connection with the postal worker assault and the photo of Kerbie and the mechanic at that scene. They were also still looking into Nakita's background and the possibility of her using an alias, since the name she was using appeared to be devoid of any information.

I was still reeling from Olivia's insinuation that my mother was—or is?—living in Gladstone. This brought up a whole new series of questions, and a new twist on what I had seen in the ledger. Emily Caldwell—*Denied*. Did that mean she was attempting to leave Gladstone and come to Destiny Falls? Without dates on those pages, I had no way of knowing if that signature happened years ago or last week!

As soon as I returned home, I spent time digging through the papers in the box to see if I might uncover some dated documents, but nothing yet. Most of the papers seemed to be normal ferry documents, but I still had a lot to look through.

I also scanned a few more old newspaper issues, but mainly saw bland features about community residents, activities, sports, and the local real estate market.

My mind was spinning, so I packed up and went to bed early. I expected a night of tossing and turning was ahead of me.

~ ~ ~

"Someone's looking mighty pretty this morning. Got a hot date?"

"Geeze! Latifa!" I jumped and spun around. "Don't sneak in on me when I'm dressing in my closet!"

"Tee hee hee. Why not? It's the utmost fun." If cats could smirk, I was sure that was what she was doing. *"So spill it, sister. All dressed up and didn't ask for my help."* She continued in a sing-song voice, *"Someone has a secret."*

"I'm just going to visit Han with Axel and Grandmother," I said.

"Ohhh. Juuust going to visit the hunky Henry Golding lookalike. So, you juuuust decided to dress up all pretty. And you juuuuust decided to sneak out of here without telling me?"

The blush that crept up my face threatened to give me away, so I turned away from my cat. She could move fast when she wanted to, and she darted between my legs and turned around to sit in front of me. She tilted her head to the side. *"Ummm humm. I think somebody's in loooove."*

"I am not in love, Latifa."

"A very heavy case of like, then?" She wiggled her little eyebrows.

I was not going to have this conversation with my cat. I distracted her by asking her where Chanel and Lola were. Worked like a charm.

I had some time before meeting up with Axel and Grandmother for our trip to see Han, so I settled in to catch up on work and e-mail. I hadn't done that in two days, which wasn't like me at all. I was in the process of touching base with a few writers about our schedule for the next issue of *Natural Living* when my eye caught on an e-mail from Luna. It had the subject line: *Marshmallow Fluff*. That was our secret code from college, meaning 'this is a big secret.' My heart raced and I opened her message.

Hayden, I've been so worried about you. Ever since seeing you in the mirror screaming and flailing your arms . . .

Wait, what?! I had been waving at her! And smiling widely to show her that all was well. Apparently, my pantomime skills needed a lot of work.

> *I've been Googling alternate worlds and magic mirrors and even went to the actual library! I keep running into the same matches—basically things like Alice in Wonderland and Narnia—though that's a wardrobe, not a mirror. I even re-watched that Star Trek episode when Picard goes to an alternate world and lives a whole life there. You're not going to do that, are you? Disappear for a whole life, get married, and have children, grow old, and then come back as young you all over again??? I found a few other old novels and movie scenes with enchanted mirror plot-lines. And well, you know, a couple of fairy tales like the Beast's window to the outside world and Snow White's fairest of them all stuff, but so far, I haven't learned anything that will help me get you out.*
>
> *I hope our secret subject line will give this message a chance at getting through to you without putting you in danger. Is someone watching your e-mail account? Can you reach me to tell me what to do to help you get out? Please try—I want to get you back home! I miss you and I'm so worried about you. You are so not in Denmark, are you?*

My throat tightened and I tried to swallow. My eyes filled with tears and I felt one slip down my cheek. My friend had not been so afraid that she'd run away and abandoned me as I'd thought. She was trying to get me back.

It also was a shock that the DF Satellite let

her message through. Any magic that powerful would not be tricked by a fancy subject line. So, for whatever reason, it was allowed. I hoped that my reply would make it through as well.

I spent the next hour writing and erasing a reply to Luna. I wanted it to be exactly right. I'd tell her just enough to calm her down and let her know I was okay. I would leave out the magic of the town and the house. And I wouldn't say anything about the murders or mysteries that had occurred since I arrived, of course. I'd be a little lighthearted so she wouldn't be concerned. And I wouldn't expound on all that I'd learned about mirrors and portals and such. Also, I thought I'd better leave out my family, even though they were such a big part of all this. I feared if I said too much, my message would become undeliverable. Finally, I had a message that felt perfect.

> *Hi Luna!*
>
> *I was so happy to get your note! When you saw me, I was not screaming or afraid. I was waving and trying to put on a very happy face. It surprised me to hear that it looked like a grimace of panic. I'm so sorry I scared you!*
>
> *The story of where I am and how I got here is complicated. It's unbelievable, but 100 percent true. It would take hours to tell you everything, so I'm just going to give you some important highlights.*
>
> *You are correct. I'm not in Denmark. Sorry about that, but it was the only way to let you know I*

was fine without explaining the very weird experience I am dealing with.

You better sit down for this next bit. Well, I imagine you're at your computer and sitting down, but you know what I mean.

You already saw that the mirror in my room is enchanted. Well, you could say I fell 'through the looking glass' and landed in a different world. Yes, I know that sounds farfetched. The world on the other side of that mirror is marvelous (nothing like the Alice experience!)—it's very much like home in many ways. I am staying in a beautiful home with a family of kind, gracious people.

The weirdest thing about the mirror is that I have no idea how it works. I can't leave here unless it sends me back.

Communication from here is spotty. I've sent you many e-mails and texts and tried to reach you by phone, only to have the connection dropped or messages bounce. I am very much hoping that you receive this. If so, maybe we can both continue to monitor the mirrors and try to see each other again.

I think this might be way too much for Nana and Granana to handle, so let's keep this between us until we figure it out, okay? I think it's best to keep the Denmark cover story for now.

I miss you, my friend. I hope we can be together again soon.

Love and hugs to you,
Hayden

I reread my note. Well, it wasn't as perfect as the first time I read it, but I felt it was good enough. The situation was so ridiculously absurd that there was no way to soften the blow. I hit 'send.'

27

Han's home was not what I expected. That was not a new concept here in Destiny Falls, I realized. Since he was so James Bond-ish, I was expecting sleek, modern, black glass, and chrome. Instead, I pulled up to a stunning, contemporary house with a rock and wood exterior. A wrap-around porch hugged the front of the house. Four rock pillars guarded the front entry, softened by long, white, accent lights. The deck transitioned into a gazebo at the far end. A row of neat white stones edged a freshly mown lawn, accented with ferns and ornamental trees. Bushes burst with small, white roses. It was lovely.

Instead of sitting in the car while I waited for Axel and Eleanor to arrive from their business meeting, I parked and walked up onto the porch.

I inched closer and peeked into the window. The interior of the home had a clean, minimalist appearance. Decorated in muted grays and forest green, the furnishings had smooth, symmetrical shapes. A slate fireplace highlighted the room with plants accenting both sides. The fireplace mantle featured several artistically cultivated bonsai trees. Gorgeous landscapes and wildlife photos dotted the walls, and I wondered if Han had taken any of them.

I was focused on my—cough, cough—investigation. Okay, fine. My spying. So, when Han's smiling face suddenly appeared on the other side of the window, I jumped back two feet.

Han opened the door and laughed. "Hi, Hayden. Or should I say booooo!" He raised his one uncasted arm and wiggled his fingers. He seemed to think this was our thing now—him unintentionally scaring me.

I sputtered, "Oh, hi! Was waiting for Axel and Eleanor and, umm, I just, umm . . ."

He laughed and gave me a quick hug. "It's okay, hon. Your high level of curiosity is one of the reasons I like you."

Did he just call me hon? As in honey? I liked that. One of the reasons he liked me? I enjoyed that comment, too.

"Come on in. You can scope out the rest of the house from an inside viewpoint."

"Ha ha. Thanks. You look really good." Then I blushed and stammered some more, "I mean, umm, you look like you're recovering well."

Han seemed to enjoy my embarrassing blunders, by the look of his smile and the dimples that emerged on his cheeks. He appeared to be holding back an outright laugh. He motioned me inside with his one good arm.

He really did look good, though! His relaxed black sweatpants were matched with a rather tight, black T-shirt that showed off his muscular physique. His jet-black hair appeared wet from a shower. His feet were bare. I normally hated looking at people's bare feet, but his were nice. The overall look was so darn sexy.

I pulled my eyes away from his feet and, of course, saw that he was watching me give him the once-over. Could I embarrass myself any more? I'd give him credit. He said nothing, just looked in my eyes and grinned.

"Wow, your home is so beautiful," I said, changing my focus from his appearance to his home.

The floor plan was bright and open. The main room flowed seamlessly into the kitchen. A white island and light gray, quartz countertops were perfectly balanced with pale wood cabinets and square, lantern-shaped, pendant lights. The same pale wood surfaces disguised the refrigerator and freezer, I assumed so as not to disrupt the balance and beauty of the space.

Soft piano music was coming through hidden speakers throughout the home, adding a classy touch to the ambiance, and making me wonder about the piano I saw in an alcove off the living room. I let the music wrap itself around me and realized Han was still watching me. Our eyes met and there was a moment of intimate connection. I remembered that gentle kiss in the park.

The spell was broken when two women came around the corner into the kitchen. They resembled Han, and the two of them almost looked like twins, so they had to be his sisters. They saw him standing there and rushed over.

"Hannie! What are you doing up?" They led him over to the sofa, urging him to sit. They grabbed his ankles and put his (sexy, bare) feet up on the footstool.

"Hey, girls! Calm down. I'm capable of answering a door and greeting my guest." He said it with a laugh. It gave me a glimpse of the close relationship they shared.

He turned toward me. "Hayden, if you haven't already guessed, these two mother hens are my sisters, Eva and Yanay. Girls, this is Hayden."

I said hello to them, my smile lit from the feeling of warmth I felt from being with Han and his family.

"It's so nice to meet you, Hayden. I'm Yanay," said the slightly taller sister. In true Destiny Falls tradition, she gave me a brief welcoming hug.

"Welcome to Han's recovery central! I'm Eva." A warm hug followed. "Han's forever taking care of us. Now it's our turn to take care of him— even when he objects."

The doorbell rang and the sisters both said, "I'll get it!" They wandered over to the front door. I could tell by how they said hello, and the familiar hugs all around, that they already knew my grandmother and Axel. If they weren't close to Eleanor, I doubt she'd be instantly huggable. Also, Axel and Grandmother seemed casually comfortable in the house, so it appeared they'd been at Han's home before.

I got up and greeted my brother and grandmother with my own hugs. They said hello to Han and asked how he was feeling. I could tell he didn't like the attention on his recovery. He said he was fine and changed the subject.

The sisters offered everyone something to drink. Then they brought out several trays of appetizers and laid out the food, drinks, plates, and napkins on the counter.

The five of us had a wonderful visit. Axel and my grandmother had another appointment, so they left together. The girls and I walked them to the door and said our goodbyes. When we turned back around, Han was asleep on the sofa.

Yanay whispered, "He needs the rest more than he knows. Hayden, can you stay a while? We can sit outside in the gazebo and let Han sleep."

"That sounds wonderful."

Yanay gathered up a tray of snacks and Eva refreshed our tea. The three of us gathered outside in the gazebo.

"It's so nice to get to know you, Hayden," said Yanay. "Han speaks very highly of you."

"Yep. Over, and over, and over," chuckled Eva.

"It's rare for him to be so taken with someone," said Yanay. "He's a very private person and doesn't let many into his bubble."

"I feel honored."

"Oh, you should. Han is an amazing person. I know he's my brother, but he's truly a special human being. When he cares for someone, he's the most devoted, honest man you could imagine. You can count on him for anything," said Yanay.

"And we do," said Eva. "It's nice for us to have this chance to do something for him. He fights the care tooth and nail since he's such a care-giver himself. It's hard for him to be on the other side."

I sipped my tea and allowed their words to settle. I had the feeling earlier that Han was unique and was finding that to be truer than I realized.

"So, Hayden. Tell us about the *Observer*. We hear you're the new editor and the paper will soon be online," said Yanay.

I told the girls all about the paper, which led to my story about the camera and taking photos with Han. Oops. I hadn't meant to bring the conversation back around to Han, but it just happened.

I looked around at the yard. "The landscaping here is wonderful, and this gazebo is perfect. I'd be sitting out here every day."

"Han does all the landscaping, you know. He works in the yard and around the house to relax. He works on those little bonsai trees too," said Eva. "Not my idea of fun, but he enjoys it. And his job can become incredibly stressful; he needs the release."

"I didn't realize that insurance investigation was so stressful," I said.

The sisters looked at each other, and Eva nodded. "Right. Insurance investigation."

"What was that look?" I asked.

"That's not something we have the right to tell," said Yanay. "When the time is right, you can ask Han about his work."

Just what I needed. More mystery. It sounded like Han was still a puzzle to solve, but one I'd happily unravel. I left his home feeling full of hope. I felt closer to him than ever, and I had made two new friends.

I was planning to stop by Poppy's Extravaganza and make my first pitch for a newspaper ad. Then, I'd head to the *Observer* office for more old-newspaper research on my ever-growing list of weird things.

28

It was cold and raining in Poppy's Camping & Hiking Extravaganza. I laughed out loud. It was cold and raining *inside* her store! There were umbrella stands just inside, filled with umbrellas of every size and color. There were racks of rain boots, coats, vests, scarves, gloves, and hats. These were all under cover, so shoppers could browse before facing the elements. Yes, that's correct. Before facing the elements *inside the store*, because outside was the same sunny weather as always.

I helped myself to a clear, plastic, bubble umbrella that covered my head and shoulders but provided a full-surround viewing window, and a pair of black rain boots covered in cats that slipped right over my shoes. Hmm. Figured I'd buy these. They would be perfect for rainy day walks. If it ever rained. And the purpose of the event was immediately clear.

The entire store was a living, breathing advertisement for everything necessary for walking, hiking, and camping in cold or rainy weather. A shopper wouldn't have to wonder if a certain tent would keep them dry on a cold, rainy, windy day. They'd just wander over to the cold, rainy, windy corner of the store and walk through a group of full-size tents to gauge their wind protection and dryness. Inside each tent, they would find a variety of sleeping bags and pads for an assessment of their warmth and comfort. Amazing and brilliant.

A walking rainbow was approaching me, and I knew in an instant it had to be Poppy. She was wearing a brilliant, red rain hat with an oversized bill over her forehead. Her jacket was like something a kindergartener would wear with an eye-catching pop of bright orange. Upon closer inspection, I realized it was a rather high-tech hiking jacket, albeit in a unique color. Her rain pants were bold yellow with a florescent white stripe down the sides. Bright green rain boots finished off the look. I bet she could wade through a pond in those and still have dry feet.

Poppy approached with a friendly smile. She somehow managed to hug me, even through my big, round umbrella and her excessively large hat.

"Hello, Hayden!" she said. "It's so good to see you. Hey, those boots are darling on you!"

"I love them. Think I'll buy the boots and this clever umbrella, too," I told her. "How are you?"

"Oh, I'm always great," Poppy said. "Life is too short to be anything else."

"What a wonderful philosophy. I'm going to write that down and remember it."

A man rolled by in a wheelchair, wearing a colorful rain poncho that covered him from top to toe, including the arms and back of his chair. It was a perfect fit. He gave Poppy a thumbs up, said thank you, and rolled over to one of the cash registers to pay.

"Wow, you've thought of everything," I said.

"I hope so. If you're planning to venture out into the mountains or visit the rainy islands, it's important to be prepared."

Hmm. The rainy islands, did she say? So, the sunny environment here in Destiny Falls was not repeated on all the other islands. That was new.

Poppy and I chatted for a bit while she pointed out some interesting things in the store. She enjoyed showing me the pet section with rain gear for dogs, cats, and even horses.

"How are things at the *Observer*?" Poppy asked. "Getting closer to the first edition?"

Ah! *A perfect opening, thank you Poppy*. Sales had not been my forte, and I always felt uncomfortable asking for money, even if the advertising was a mutual benefit.

"I'm getting closer. My first goal is to sign up local businesses for regular advertising. You have the most amazing events here. Would you consider running a regular ad series?"

"That's a wonderful idea, Hayden. Count me in. Just e-mail me the info and specs." She handed me a business card that she pulled out of one of her many pockets. "Here's my e-mail address."

That was easy. I hoped that other local business owners would be just as eager to place ads.

I paid for my umbrella, boots, and a great pair of gloves and headed outside into the sunshine. I deposited my bags into the car and walked the short block to the *Observer* office.

The same three men from before were stationed outside my new office. It made me uneasy to see them there again. Why did they hang around in front of my window? Were they waiting for me to arrive or were they spying on my office?

What were their names, again? I pulled up the notes app on my phone and scrolled back. Ah, right. Lester, the mustached pharmacist, Vito from the hardware store, and Archibald, the accurately named bald owner of Time Travels On, the antique store next door to me.

That's when I relaxed. Of course. The bench was in front of my place, which was right next door to his shop. It would make sense that it would be their gathering spot. I let out a breath I didn't even realize I'd been holding. *Nothing nefarious here, Hayden, calm down.*

"Good afternoon!" I called out as I approached.

"Hey, hey! Hello there, Hayden," said Vito. "How ya doing, girly?"

"Afternoon, ma'am," said Archibald.

Oy. Between the ma'am and the girly, these guys made me wince, but I disguised it with a grin.

Lester winked and smiled, his gold tooth

drawing my attention in a mildly disturbing way. He gave me that familiar salute.

"How are you all today?" I asked.

There were murmurs of *good* and *fine*.

"Been poking into people's business, yet?" asked Lester, snickering. He had an odd sense of humor, and he obviously wasn't tired of that joke.

"Don't pick on the girl," said Archibald.

"When's that paper startin' back up?" asked Vito. "We was just sayin' it'll be good to have a paper to run our coupons in. People 'round here like their coupons, you know?"

Well, that was just way too easy.

I spent the next fifteen minutes getting commitments from them to run ads in the paper.

Prying myself away from the local businessmen's club took a bit of finesse, but I finally managed. They thought it was fantastic that I was going inside to work on the first edition of the paper. I didn't have the heart to tell them I had other, more pressing, issues to address first.

Archibald, Lester, and Vito. What an eccentric trio.

I pulled up the photo I had taken of the ledger page of names. I again felt a weird jolt of emotion when I saw my mother's name on the list. So very strange. I figured that I'd check the newspaper directory of past articles to see if any of the names popped up. That might clue me in to the dates that these pages were created and perhaps some piece of information that explained the ferry trips.

I started entering the names one by one and, so far, had no matches. Wait a minute. I looked at the last two columns on the page: *Agent*: K, V, A. *Paid*: L, M. I circled the V, the A, and the L. Archibald, Lester, and Vito? My gran always used to say, "There are no coincidences." I never believed that, but I had to admit, this was suspicious.

I couldn't tell Jaxson about the ledgers, but I could tell him I felt something was odd about those three men. Maybe a little nudge would get him to investigate, just in case. I texted him a quick note.

> *Hey Jax. Just something to look into.*
> *Three local businessmen hang out in*
> *front of the* Observer. *Something's just*
> *a bit off. Maybe check them out?*

> *Of course. But what do you*
> *mean off? Names, please.*

> *Nothing specific. Just a feeling. Lester the*
> *pharmacist, Vito from the hardware store,*
> *and Archibald owner of Time Travels On,*
> *the antique store next door to me.*

> *OK, sure. Will do a quick check.*

If you have details let me know.

Now that I knew Jaxson would check out the three men, I could proceed with my list of names. I entered them one by one until my eyes were blurry.

Finally! I found a match.

There was an article about a young woman named Claire-Marie Renavand—an approved name on the list. She was originally from France and moved here for a ballet opportunity. The article was only five years old, and Claire-Marie was twenty-seven in the article! Maybe I was zeroing in on the date range for the log. I scanned the rest of the article and lost a bit of hope. She moved here with her mother, also named Claire-Marie Renavand. There was a chance this narrowed down the date on the log to recent times though. Hers was a unique name, here in the States. As long as there wasn't a grandmother or great-grandmother with the same name. If there was, then this told me nothing. Was the name on the log the daughter or the mother? I wish I knew. There was no reference to the ferry or boat travel in the article that would give me any insight, but I knew that five years ago she lived in Destiny Falls.

I snapped a photo of the article and looked up her name in the local directory. Bingo! She, or at least someone by that name, owned the ballet studio in town. I placed a call and got a voicemail. I left a message. My maps app did not appear to work in Destiny Falls, no surprise. However, the street name seemed familiar. I thought I'd drive around and see if I could find the ballet studio.

I finally found the studio and, oddly, it was across the street from the library's new location. I'd take that as a sign that a visit to the library was in order. When I finished here, I'd stop over there. The studio door was open, but I didn't see anyone inside.

"Hello?" I called out.

A voice came from a back room. "Just a moment," called a woman with a French accent.

I wandered around the studio while I waited. It was clean and pretty, but it was very tiny. Just enough for a class of maybe ten students at a time.

A beautiful woman emerged from the back. She was in her mid-thirties, I'd guess—the right age for the woman from the article. She was obviously a dancer, with her slim figure, long legs encased in footless, black tights, and hair twisted up into a bun.

"May I help you?" she asked with a pleasant smile.

"Are you Claire-Marie Renavand?"

"Yes, that is me. I am the owner of this studio. Are you interested in dance lessons?" she asked.

"No, not at this time. I'm Hayden, a reporter

from the *Observer*." I thought saying a reporter was less intimidating than editor, and it was one of my many hats. I reached out to shake her hand, but she didn't take it, so I let it fall to my side.

"I'm following up on a past article. I'm wondering if you can tell me anything about the Destiny Falls ferry and a trip that was taken some time ago."

Her smile disappeared, and her face turned hard. "I can tell you nothing."

"Have you ever taken a trip on the ferry?"

"You sound like my mother with her obsession over the ferry and her search for youth and beauty. I never want to hear of this ferry again!" She spit on her nice, clean, wood floor.

She was turning red and looked pinched and angry, but I had to try one more question. "I'm sorry this upsets you. Perhaps I could talk with your mother?"

"My mother. She is gone. Poof!" She snapped her fingers. "The promise blinded her. She saw nothing else. She left behind a daughter with no mother. And no money. I do not wish to discuss this. Please, leave my studio and leave me in peace." She gestured to the door. When I didn't move, she walked to the front and yanked open the door so hard it banged against the wall. In an angry voice, she said, "Au revoir!"

I don't know much French, but I did know that meant goodbye.

29

From the time I was in kindergarten, library day was my favorite day of the week. I would wake up early and just about drag Nana or Granana all the way on our walk there. I couldn't wait to get to the building and embrace all the new wonders that awaited me. There was no feeling quite like my empty blue box and shelf upon shelf of opportunities to fill it.

I never stuck to the tiny child's corner of the library. Oh, no, not me. I would uncover hidden wonders everywhere. I've never forgotten the day I found the oversized book section. These were all the books that were too large to fit anywhere else. The subjects were endless, and most of these extra-large books contained pictures, maps, or diagrams. Different breeds of dogs. Treasures found in pyramids. Undersea creatures. Sculptures and paintings. Tattoos through the ages. Distinctive home designs. Classic cars. Photo tours of faraway places. People who changed the world. *National Geographic* and Audubon image collections. That's just the tip of the iceberg. The oversized book section was my favorite place: a journey for the eyes.

I loved reminiscing about those times and my marvelous library. What I thought was the pinnacle of library visits was sea level compared to the Destiny Falls library! Not only were all books ever written available to patrons, but the library itself was a wondrous experience. Nearly every time I visited was a new and eye-popping adventure. Today was one of those adventures. The theme: Birds.

The entrance of the library today had a double-door system. I realized why they had arranged it this way as soon as I stepped out of the entry area into the main lobby. The foyer was now the largest aviary I'd ever seen. Tall, slim trees filled the room. The ceiling of the building looked to be a hundred feet up. I looked through the canopy of trees to the very top, which resembled the crest of a golden birdcage.

Birds of every size, color, and breed flew happily from tree to tree. I spotted tiny hummingbirds and a large bald eagle. I saw a pelican, colorful parrots, toucans, and a bright green quetzal with a long, wispy tail. A pair of peacocks were wandering on the ground. The sounds were a mixed melody of chirping, tweeting, and an occasional squawk.

As usual, there were bookcases set up around the perimeter with books on the theme. Amusingly, they were under a plastic dome. I assume this was to protect them from bird droppings. There were books about birds, birdhouses, bird art, birdwatching, ancient birds, and bird training—yes, bird training. There were movies, audiobooks, and birdsong recordings. Children in the craft corner were gluing colorful feathers onto headbands and wearing their creations. The colorful parrot in their corner was making the kids laugh with funny, bird-like words and opera-like singing.

I realized my friendly camera was around my neck, so I took photos of the displays and some close-ups of the birds. I got a great picture of the children and their feathery headbands.

I left the foyer and made my way through another set of double doors into the main library area and stopped to stare. "Oh, my!" escaped my lips as I took in the vision. I snapped a few photos for a feature in the *Observer*.

My favorite aspects of the library remained the same as always—the multitude of bookshelves, home to thousands of volumes, the cozy reading areas, and the long study tables. But today, up near the ceilings, waves of thousands of origami birds floated through the entire building. A spiral of them whooshed up the middle of the grand staircase. I assumed that wire held them up, but possibly it was a wisp of magic. They were in every color—groups of birds blending in a rhythmic pattern. First, a flock of light blue, then progressively getting darker along the line, up to deep midnight blue. A pale green group followed, evolving into dark emerald, then purple shades, red, orange, yellow, and white.

Surely, no human being had folded thousands of little origami birds—it had to be magic.

As I looked closer, I realized that every single bird carried a one-word inspirational message. *Wander. Create. Fly. Dream. Imagine. Appreciate.* The bird creations moved lightly in a softly flowing string of colors, almost like an aurora borealis made of delicate, colorful, paper doves. The effect was mesmerizing.

I was so busy looking up that I didn't notice Edna approach. Next thing I knew she was shoulder to shoulder with me, looking up at the colorful chains of origami birds.

"Beautiful, isn't it?" she whispered.

"Oh, so beautiful," I agreed. We watched together quietly for a few minutes, then she pulled out her key and dangled it in the air. I followed her up the stairs to the private, historic, book room.

Looking around the space, I opened myself to the will of the library. It usually seemed to know what I needed and had eventually directed me to the right choice. I stood perfectly still for a good five minutes but received no supernatural message. Oh, well. It was worth a try. I wandered around browsing the shelves.

The enormous globe that appeared on my last visit was nowhere to be found; neither was the unique aquarium table. Even without these things, the room was a joy. It embraced me with its warm woods, comfortable stuffed chairs, ornate light fixtures, and shelves filled with books. There were several elaborate birdcages filled with finches and canaries. Smaller birds with smaller voices for this smaller room.

Today, for the first time ever, I saw Edna enter the room carrying a tray of tea and cookies. That tray always appeared when I was here, and I had assumed it was Edna who brought it. Now I saw I was correct. Or at least on this visit I was correct.

"Thank you so much! It's very kind of you," I said.

"My pleasure, Hayden."

I sat at the table and poured a cup of tea. Snacking on a cookie, I scanned the pile of books someone—something?—had pulled out for me. I tried to decide where to start. As I was debating where to begin, I realized that Edna was still in the room.

She closed the door to the hallway and then came over to my table. She sat across from me. "Ever since your last visit, when the globe showed you Gladstone, you've been on my mind. I've been doing some research. Once I began to learn more, I even accessed the library's hidden web, which I've only done once before, since sometimes you find things that you're better off not knowing. I have discovered some stories and myths that you might like to hear."

"Yes, please!" I answered, sitting up tall in my chair, ready to listen.

"I'll be happy to share what I've learned, but keep in mind, none of this has ever been confirmed. It's all just legends, myths, and rumors."

"Good enough for me!" I opened a note page on my phone and eagerly awaited her stories.

Edna reached over and snagged a cookie. She seemed to think where to start.

"I've learned that in many ways, Gladstone is a direct opposite of Destiny Falls. When our climate is most usually warm and sunny, theirs is cold, cloudy, and snowy. Where people here tend to be friendly and kind, people in Gladstone are often untrustworthy and aloof. While touches of enchantment here are blessings of wonder"—she gestured around the library—"the magic that appears there is of a darker type."

I thought about the people in the ferry line that I had seen. Most had items for a day at the beach, but I had seen cars of people with winter clothes and ski gear. The weather part of her story rang true. Well, true if the ferry was headed to wintry Gladstone.

"It doesn't sound like an appealing place to visit. Why is it so elusive? People seem to know nothing about it."

"I believe that's part of the veil it created. You must understand that while we believe that Gladstone exists, it's not a typical island, port, or city. It's . . . how shall I say this? It's almost a mirage. We have heard it is there, but if you try to reach it, you may find it doesn't exist. Until it does.

For only some people. There appears to be a power that decides which people reach the island and which are turned away. Most leave from here on their journey, only to find themselves back at the Destiny Falls ferry terminal with no understanding of how the circular trip occurred."

"Wow, that's extremely odd, even for Destiny Falls!" I shook my head.

"It gets even weirder," she said. "I've read that some people do reach Gladstone. But they find only a small, typical port town—much like Destiny Falls or any harbor town. The major differences being the weather, the less sociable population, and a general feeling of . . . how do I explain? Creepiness, I guess. It has been rumored to be an unsettling place, and people become eager to leave and try to shorten their trip. Sometimes, though, it's been said that once Gladstone gets its hooks in you, it doesn't permit you to leave."

"But then why do people try to visit Gladstone? Is it because these facts aren't well known? It seems that the people I've asked don't know this."

"In part," Edna continued. "They either don't know, or they are too afraid to talk about it."

I thought about that. Whenever I brought up Gladstone, people looked uncomfortable and often changed the subject.

Edna had more to tell. "There is a colossal lure that draws people there," she began. "There are stories of enchanted lakes that have magical properties, though it's not clear what the magic is or how you gain access to it. I've never heard whether you have to swim in the water or drink it or just stand at the shore."

This story intrigued me since I'd had my own magical waterfall experience at Twin Falls Lake. Most people only see one waterfall. I saw two, and the second was magical. I wouldn't have believed her story otherwise. My experience was amazing and inspiring. But if Gladstone was a place of opposites . . . I shuddered.

I was waiting to see if she had information about the lake with the so-called fountain of youth that I'd read about in the window-seat book.

"The most intriguing myth is that one particular lake holds a fountain of youth. That's just the common title for such a thing. I've never heard it to be an actual fountain. I've never heard how it provides this so-called magic."

Ah! A second source for this myth. I puffed out a breath. "That would be a powerful magnet."

"It's said to be almost impossible to find. The rumored location is at the summit of one of the snowy mountains. Many people who make it to the island and hike up a mountain are never seen again. It's assumed to be a challenging hike through treacherous terrain and untold dangers."

I thought about her words for a minute. "But the promise to be forever young would cause people to take that risk, wouldn't it?"

"That's true. Some people who hear of this

magic desperately try to get there. Often, it is people who fear death or aging that find the appeal of being ageless worth the risk of finding it."

The pieces were coming together. Did the ferry travel to Gladstone? Were the large dollar amounts on the ledger related to this so-called fountain of youth? Was the box I received from the captain a key to figuring out the mystery of Gladstone? Was this the heart of the danger the captain warned me of? The reason for her death?

I recalled the dancer's anger and her comments about her mother. She'd said something about her mother's search for youth and beauty. And she said she had disappeared. Leaving her daughter alone and penniless.

The idea that my own mother was, or could still be, in Gladstone worried me. Was my mother one of those self-absorbed people on a quest for youthfulness at all costs?

30

One minute I was in the library with Edna, and the next I was back at Caldwell Crest and in my room. I wasn't sure if this was magic or if I had just been in a complete daze, kind of like when I used to drive to work in Seattle, and I'd zone out and be in the parking lot without much memory of the drive. I was trying to process everything that Edna had told me about Gladstone and tie it to the various strange things that had been happening.

My brain was in such a muddle that I tried to unwind in my yoga room. I was halfway through a sun salutation when I caught a flicker of movement in the now oval shaped mirror. I rushed over and was beyond happy to see Luna folding her laundry. How could such a mundane task bring tears to my eyes and an ache in my heart?

Typical of Luna, she was swaying and bopping along as she folded. I didn't need to hear it to know that she had her music on loud. Her carefree approach to her housework gave me a warm, fuzzy feeling.

I stood at the mirror for the longest time, just watching her and willing her to turn around. Finally, she did. This time there was no screaming and running, thankfully. Instead, she popped out her earbuds and began joyfully talking, gesturing wildly as she spoke.

I shook my head and made talking gestures with my hand, mouthing the words, 'I can't hear you.' Then I pulled my phone out of my pocket and pointed to it.

I dialed Luna's number and hoped. So many times I had tried to reach her, only to have the call drop before she even had a chance to pick up. I saw her run over to her purse and pull out her phone. I held my breath.

"Hello?" Luna's voice was quiet and tentative—not like her at all.

"Oh my God! Luna! It's you! I can't believe it! Hi, Luna!" I was stumbling over my words in my surprise.

"Hayden! It's you!" She was laughing. "I was hoping every day that you'd be back!"

Then we were both laughing and talking over each other. She walked over to the mirror, and it was almost as if we were together again. She moved closer to the mirror and blew me a kiss. That got me laughing again, which felt so darn good.

"Before I explain things, there's something important. If the room starts to look wavy or faded, or if you see a flash of bright light, you need to hit the deck. Lie down on the floor and crawl out of there. Don't get close to the mirror again. That seems to be a sign that you're going to be pulled into the other side, and once you're here, you can't get out. So, you got that?"

"Got it." She pulled a stool over to the dresser and sat down. "So, talk, my friend. Tell me everything!"

Well, once I started talking, I couldn't stop. I explained how I had landed in Destiny Falls and what I found here. I told her about my newfound family. I told her about the unbelievable stores and the library. I told her about the *Observer*. I told her—a tiny bit—about Jaxson and Han. And then, once I was on a roll, it all came spilling out. Well, not all, but plenty.

I told Luna about the mysterious ferry, the odd parallel island of Gladstone, and the box that was mailed to me by the now-dead ferry captain. I told her about seeing my mother's name on the page. I even told her the story of the weird encounter with the ballet dancer. Over two hours later, I finally took a breath.

"Hayden, you listen to me," Luna started in the most serious voice I'd ever heard from her. "You may be in more danger than you think. You're in a place that doesn't follow normal human rules. This all sounds very scary. I think that the potential for danger could be much more than you can handle on your own."

"I realize that," I said. "But the warnings from the ferry captain before her death have me terrified to tell anyone about her words or the box that she sent me."

"I understand. But keeping it to yourself could be worse. It sounds like you have some good people around you. I think you have to decide to trust them." Luna looked concerned. She looked down at the floor in deep thought and chewed her thumbnail. She was quiet for several minutes.

Finally, Luna looked up. "Hayden. Tell Sheriff Jaxson everything. Tell him about the box. He's law enforcement. He'll have the means to protect you. He's a Destiny Falls native. He'll know what to do."

Fear twisted in my gut. What if she was wrong?

"Luna, what if my telling someone opens up terrible trouble?"

"This will not clear up all by itself. It won't suddenly go away, and you'll have the happily ever after you always want. Action needs to be taken. You need help from people who understand that place better than you do."

I knew she was right.

"Okay. I will. When I find the right moment, I'll talk to Jaxson about everything."

"Do it soon. Promise?" Luna pressed.

"I promise."

"Umm. Hayden. Is that Sassy and two other cats behind you?"

I turned around to see the three cats huddled up on the yoga mat behind me, all of them watching me talk to Luna in the mirror.

Meow. Meeeeow. *"Did that sound sufficiently cat-like?"* Latifa asked in that telepathic voice that only I could hear.

"Yes, it is! It's Sassy!" I answered.

"That's your cue, Duckie. Tell her I'm now to be called Princess Latifa."

Meeeeeow!

I knew if I didn't say something, my cat would become obnoxious. "I've started calling her Latifa now," I said.

"Why?" Luna asked.

"It's a long story." I quickly cut that conversation short by moving on to introductions to the other cats.

"This gorgeous, white Persian is my grandmother's cat, Chanel. And this tiny, black fluffball is our newest addition, Lola." I picked her up and held her close to the mirror.

"My goodness. She is adorable!" said Luna. "I'm happy to see you have some feline company."

"Oh, you have no idea," I mumbled under my breath.

31

I tossed and turned all night. My joy at talking to Luna kept being interrupted by the feeling of fear in my gut. Luna was right. The secrets I'd been keeping about the ferry captain and the box could be more dangerous to keep than to tell.

I finally gave up on sleep and got out of bed just before six. I crept out of the quiet house and took a slow jog through town to Vessie's café. I arrived before she opened and spotted a large black-and-white cat sitting outside the door.

"Hello, kitty. Are you waiting for Vessie to open, too?" I stroked her soft fur and noticed a tag on her collar. "So, you're Vessie's cat, Marshmallow. You are a pretty one."

I walked over and sat on the bench that overlooked the harbor. Marshmallow followed me over and jumped up beside me. The two of us enjoyed the morning sunshine. It wasn't long before I heard the bells jingle above the café door.

"Good morning, you two!" Vessie's cheerful voice rang out. She walked over to the bench and gifted me with one of her warm hugs. "Shop's open! Ready to come in now?"

Latifa had said Marshmallow called the café the pink palace. And for good reason. This morning it was as pink as ever. While the basic structure of the café always remained the same, and the dominant color was always pink, the décor was often slightly different, sometimes radically different. Today, the theme was polka dots. The walls were dark pink and covered with huge, white dots, while the ceiling was white with small, pink dots. The floor was a sea of tiny, round tiles that were pink, white, and gold. There was a ribbon of ivy over the front door and around the perimeter of the room near the ceiling, speckled with dots of tiny white and pink flowers. The ever-present butterflies were flittering here and there on the ivy. The room was bright and cheery.

"Are you meeting Jaxson this morning?" she asked.

I jerked my head up from the menu and looked at her. "No. Why?" Did she know something? Why would she think I was meeting Jaxson?

"Um, because he's just walking in the door?" She chuckled. "Hi, Jax! Coffee?"

"Yes, please. Morning, Hayden. Want some company?" he asked.

"Of course!"

Jaxson sat in the booth across from me. Vessie brought his coffee and a cup of tea for me. She took our orders, and then wandered back to the kitchen.

This was my chance. I could tell him about the box and the warning now. I took a deep breath.

"Interested in hearing some news about the ferry captain case?" he asked. "I expect you'll want to write about this in the paper as soon as the case is closed. I'd ask that you hold off until then. But we seem to be getting closer."

"Yes. And you're right. It would be a great cover story for my first issue. I suspect murder is big news in a small town."

"Who told you Destiny Falls is a small town?" he asked.

"Really? You just have to look around. It's pretty obvious."

"Hmm. Right," he said, nodding. But he didn't sound convinced. Oh, seriously? Was there more mystery surrounding this place? I was about to ask, but he launched into his update.

"Olivia was right. Nakita and her husband separated about a year ago. They both started dating other people. He moved away soon after. For whatever reason, they didn't file divorce papers, but she was living as a divorced woman. She had her own apartment with no signs of a man living there with her. She was dating, but casually, no one in particular."

"That's pretty much what Olivia told me," I said.

"We still haven't located her estranged husband, but they separated amicably. No kids, pets, or much in the way of assets. Since he hasn't been seen in nearly a year, and we can't detect any motive there, he's an unlikely suspect."

I thought about how Oliva had started to say the husband had moved away to 'Glad' but never finished her sentence. She refused to say more, but it was clear she was going to say Gladstone. After that, she told me it was a forbidden place to travel to and a topic to be avoided. Add to that the description I'd learned from Edna about the people in Gladstone being untrustworthy and aloof. I wasn't entirely sure he should be off the list as a suspect.

Vessie came to the table with our breakfast, and we took a few minutes to chat with her. Normally, I love talking with Vessie, but my leg was bouncing around under the table. I wanted to hear the rest of Jaxson's update. And then, I would tell him about the box.

"Well, I don't want to keep you from your breakfast!" Vessie said. "Enjoy!"

Jaxson took a bite of his omelet and chewed. Then he returned to our conversation.

"Oh, on another topic. I'm doing a background check on your three business neighbors. Nothing out of the ordinary has showed up yet, but there are some gaps. They appear to have been around for a few years, but I haven't been able to figure out where they immigrated here from. Let me know if you discover anything about them, or if you can provide specifics about any odd behavior. That would give me something to go on."

"Okay, sure," I said.

"We have learned something of interest

about the ferry captain that could lead to motive and opportunity."

"Really?"

"Yeah. We've found evidence that she was involved in an illegal transport scheme. We don't know what exactly she was transporting, but we've uncovered evidence that it involved large amounts of money and that it has been going on for years."

What I said was, "Wow. That's really strange." What I was thinking was, "Holy crap!" I wondered where he had learned that information. I also speculated that what they were transporting illegally was passengers. Specifically, the people on those lists.

"And we have a saying at the office, 'Where there's big money, there's motive for murder.' Even more, we've discovered that she spent a lot of time outside of work hours with Kerbie, the helmsman, and the two mechanics, known as Gronk and Shrek. We're looking into the ferry records for their full names and backgrounds now."

I took a deep breath. This was the perfect time to tell him about the box because now it seemed even more connected to the murder than ever before.

Jaxson's phone rang. "Excuse me," he said. "Redford here. Yeah . . . Yeah . . . Copy that. On my way.

"Sorry, Hayden. Duty calls." He stood up, threw some cash on the table, gave me a quick hug, and hustled out of the café.

32

The walk back home was excruciating. I had totally missed the opportunity to tell Jaxson about the box. And now that I was beginning to understand that it was a major puzzle piece, I was regretting not telling him sooner. I couldn't really blame myself, though. I had received that frightening warning from the ferry captain. She had said it was life and death, and danger to my family. Then she was murdered. It was no joke.

However, I was new here. The Caldwell family and Sheriff Jaxson understood Destiny Falls. The unique, enchanted town and the odd people who inhabited it. It now felt like I had made the wrong decision to hide this from them.

Or had I?

Would I expose these people to danger? These people whom I'd come to care deeply about? Would telling them be like pushing a snowball down a hill that I would not be able to stop? I felt a sense of impending doom, and my stomach clenched. A trickle of sweat ran down my back, and I realized I was making fists so tight that I was digging my nails into my palms.

I needed to stop this ruminating! I had promised Luna I would tell Jaxson. So, I would. I'd try to reach him later today after he dealt with whatever sheriff's office emergency had caused him to run out of our breakfast.

~ ~ ~

I opened the door to Caldwell Crest and heard voices in the kitchen, my favorite room in the house. The warm cabin retreat-style design would never grow old for me. I could live in this kitchen and never tire of it. But this morning, I wasn't feeling that warmth as I usually did. I felt cold and worried.

I followed the cheerful sound of conversation and was glad to see my youngest brother, Cobalt was home from college. He was always a burst of joyful energy in the house and seemed to make everyone just a little happier. I assumed his being the youngest in the family was the reason for that.

"Hey, hey! Look who's here!" Cobalt sprang up from his seat, dodged the end of the counter, and leaped over to me. He gave me an enthusiastic, brotherly bear hug. "Good to see you, new sister," he said.

"Have you had breakfast?" my grandmother asked. Ever the hostess, she always made sure that those around her had something to eat and drink.

"I have eaten. But I'd love some tea, thank you."

Minutes later, I sat at the counter with a fresh cup of tea made by my always-quiet grandfather, along with some 'just in case' scones. Normally, I'd nibble on the scones, but right now my stomach was still churning.

Axel was busy in the kitchen, flipping pancakes and tending to a sizzling pan of bacon. He called a hello over his shoulder with a welcoming smile and a wave of a spatula.

The cheerful camaraderie and chatter in the kitchen ground to a halt when everyone's cell phones pinged at once. I looked down at my screen to see a group message from Indigo.

> *Sapphire is gone. Omar*
> *and I are on our way over.*
> *Be there in 5. Calling Jaxson.*

"What in the name of heaven?" Grandmother shouted. "What does she mean 'gone'?"

Grandmother pushed the buttons on her phone so hard I thought it might break. "It's gone right to voicemail."

My grandfather came to her side and put his arm around her shoulders. "She's probably talking to Jaxson. They are on their way. It's a five-minute drive. They'll explain when they get here."

A few minutes later, I heard a police siren in the distance. I realized just then how rare that sound was here. Back in Seattle, I tuned it out. In the city, there was always a reason for a police car, an aid car, or a fire truck. I realized that here, in Destiny Falls, I rarely heard or saw any of these.

We all paced the room. There were quiet

murmurs of concern and questions. One by one, everyone walked to the window to look out at the driveway. Sure enough, a couple of minutes later, Omar and Indigo's car sped up the driveway. The sheriff's vehicle, siren screaming and lights ablaze, was right behind them.

Indigo jumped out of the passenger side of the car before Omar had fully come to a stop. She didn't even bother to shut the door behind her. Omar slammed the car in park and came rushing out after her. Jaxson parked and ran up to the door behind them.

Jaxson held his hand up to the group of us. "No one talk but Omar." He turned to face Indigo's husband. "Explain what happened."

Omar was, as always, reserved and serious, but spoke quickly. "We dropped Ian off at my brother's, then went to Sapphire's home. She didn't answer multiple rings and knocks at the door, even though she was expecting us. We walked around to the back of the house to find her patio door glass broken and the door wide open. She was not in the house. We found this note on the counter."

He held a piece of paper out to Jaxson, who read it aloud in his booming sheriff-mode voice:

You have what I want. Now I have something you want. Meet me at the ferry tomorrow just before first sailing.

Don't try any funny business or she dies. I will

trade the girl for the box. Then I will get on the ferry, and she will come off. No one try to stop me.

Every voice except mine gasped in unison, "What box?"

33

There was a heartbeat of quiet while my brain and body were frozen in shock, my stomach a knot of fear. Then I forced my mouth to work.

"I have the box," I said.

"What do you mean you have the box?" Axel's voice came out in a roar. I'd never heard him raise his voice or display any anger. He was frightening when he was mad, especially because he directed it at me.

"It was delivered to me the day of the postal worker's assault."

"And you have hidden it from us? Why, Hayden?" Axel's jaw was tense, his hands were in fists, planted on his hips. Jaxson was beside him, an eerie twin of anger and frustration.

I felt numb all over, and I could barely breathe. I sucked in a ragged breath and tried to explain. "I met the ferry captain at the café. She cornered me and told me she had secrets. That she had something for me. She said if I told anyone, it would result in danger to our family. She said it was a matter of life or death."

"Do you not trust us? Did you not think we would be equipped to handle this?" Axel's face was tight and red. "And now my sister—*your sister!*—is gone."

"But . . . she said it was life or death! And then she died! Was murdered! I was terrified that if I told anyone about the box, it would mean putting all of you at risk!" I could feel tears filling my eyes, and my chest felt heavy with fear and confusion. "I've been careful."

"Careful?" Axel bit out the word. "You realize there has been a murder? And the victim sent you the box? Careful would have been you telling us what's happening. Not dropping clues like this is some Nancy Drew mystery. Go!" he yelled, pointing at the house. "Get us that box."

I rushed past the family, seeing the disappointment, fear, and anger on all their faces. I was crushed. I thought I was protecting them, but I had made everything worse. Now Sapphire was in danger! I ran up the stairs. I tore into the closet and threw the blankets and laundry aside.

I turned around to see Latifa staring at me with big, round eyes. *"Calm down, Cupcake. What's the rush?"*

"Oh, Latifa!" I cried. "I've made a huge mistake." I felt the tears dripping down my face. "Someone has kidnapped Sapphire! Kidnapped! By someone who wants this box." I pounded my fists on the box.

"I knew it was important. But I had no idea! Now she's in danger. She could be hurt! And the entire family hates me!" I sobbed.

"Honey, honey. Nobody hates you," Latifa crooned. *"Family can be mad at you and not hate*

you. Take them the box. Help them find Sapphire."

"What if someone hurts her? It will be my fault!"

"Go. Give them the box. Help them find Sapphire. Don't think about anything else."

"But . . ."

"Hayden!" Latifa's voice was deep and filled with authority. I'd never heard her use that tone of voice before. She reminded me of Grandmother. *"Take the box. Find Sapphire. Worry about the rest later."*

I brought the box downstairs and took it into the dining room, where everyone had converged. I placed it on the table.

"I'm sorry I didn't show it to you sooner, I was trying to protect—" I started, but Grandmother interrupted.

"Explanations later. Do you recall what I taught you about Caldwell women? We keep our emotions in check. We get focused. You are a Caldwell woman, are you not?"

I swallowed and nodded. She still called me a Caldwell woman, even after my failure. There was hope.

As Jaxson was the only non-family member, and a law enforcement professional, he remained unruffled in the middle of this hurricane. He stepped in and took charge. "Open the box. Tell us what you know of its arrival and its contents."

"The box was delivered right after someone attacked the mail carrier." I looked at my father and he nodded. He recalled the delivery.

"It was from the ferry office. It was packed with a mess of files and papers as if someone had overturned a drawer into it. I've been sorting everything and putting things in order."

"What have you learned from the contents?" asked Jaxson.

"Most documents pertain to the ferry travels. The most unusual are these lists of names." I pulled the files out of the box and laid them on the table. "There are several of these folders. There are about fifty pages of names. None are dated.

"The names are printed, followed by what appear to be signatures. Each name is labeled either *Approved* or *Denied,* but by whom, I don't know. All the amounts are excessively large for a ferry trip. There is a column that shows the name of an agent, and one that indicates each has been paid and to whom, but that is just labeled with initials.

"Jaxson told me this morning that he discovered the captain was involved in an illegal transport scheme. I surmised that what they were transporting illegally was passengers. Specifically, the people on these lists."

I could see Axel out of the corner of my eye. He looked furious, but he was focused and tightly contained. It made me sick to my stomach, but I continued talking.

"I have been at the library, learning more about the island of Gladstone. I believe that people would pay sizable sums to achieve the rumored magic from there. There may be a connection."

Everyone remained silent, listening. Since there was no great gasp after my bombshell about Gladstone, I surmised that they all were familiar with the myths.

"I found this note at the very bottom of the box." I placed the oddly cheerful, yellow post-it on the table and shuddered at the hastily scribbled words: *Hayden—I'm sorry. I tried. Be careful. N.*

Everyone clustered around the table. They were listening attentively and scanning the documents, though I could feel the tension in the air.

"I want to show you one other very strange finding." I glanced at my father. He was standing up, listening intently, and looking at the documents. I wasn't sure how he would handle this next piece of news. I flipped through the pages and pulled out the one I had looked at over and over again. I pointed.

"I found this name on the page. Emily Caldwell. The last column says *Denied.*"

My father fell back into the chair behind him. His eyes opened wide, and he turned ghostly white.

Eleanor turned to Leonard and spoke loudly. "Leonard. Keep your focus. We must find Sapphire. Examine your emotions on this point later."

My father shook his head, flexed his shoulders, and sat upright. With a valiant effort, his expression cleared. He looked at Jaxson. "What is the process?"

Jaxson gave each person a handful of papers and files and instructed us to read carefully and look for any clues to where they might be holding Sapphire. He said any mention of a location or address could be a lead.

"Two other things," Jaxson said, as was handing out papers. "We have suspicions about the ferry helmsman, Kerbie Gomez, and two mechanics, known as Gronk and Shrek. They are brothers, actual names Jared and Herman Serano. Keep your eye out for those names."

I was eternally grateful that he left out the reason he suspected them was based on the photo I took on the day of the package delivery. That would give the family one more reason to be furious with me.

"Also, watch for names with the initials of A, K, V, L, or M—those that are on the ledgers. Obviously, Kerbie could be the K, but that's not a given. Watch for these names also—Lester Wright, Archibald Zimmerman, and Vito Stallone." He grabbed a piece of paper and wrote down the names and initials.

"I have two officers scouting the ferry area and the general downtown area. Obviously, we can't search all of Destiny Falls, so any tips could be critical. I'll head to the ferry myself. Call me immediately with any locations mentioned and text me any addresses you find. Our goal is to find her as soon as possible. We don't want to wait until the appointed time tomorrow morning. It's to our advantage to catch the perpetrator off guard."

With that, Jaxson left to begin his search for Sapphire. We all gathered our stacks of papers and folders and took seats around the dining table.

A minute later, Cleobella entered the room, pushing a cart of sandwiches and beverages. In keeping with the somber tone of the gathering, she was dressed in relatively normal clothing. Though I did get a glimpse of her mile-long eyelashes and sky-high heels.

34

The dining room was silent, except for the shuffle of papers as we read through the files in front of us. The air was thick with worry and tension. A painful hour ticked by with not a single word spoken.

Indigo's gasp broke the silence. "I found something," she said. "It's a hand-scribbled note on the edge of the page. It says, 'Andrews group—DF to Gladstone' with a question mark."

Axel spoke up. "That could verify that Gladstone was a destination. Might be evidence of the illegal transport scheme. Let's put any papers with tips like this aside." He got up and took the page from Indigo and placed it on the far end of the table.

"Illegal transport doesn't quite define this situation," said Omar. "If Gladstone is protected by dark magic, it would prevent the transport, regardless of whether it was legal or not. I fear something wicked is behind this. Something powerful that can break through the shield."

"I thought the same thing," said Axel. "Why is this box so important? It could be the list of names. People willing to pay these high sums.

"Hayden," Axel said.

I winced at the harsh tone he put into my

name and looked up from my file.

"Have you researched the names?"

"I have." I took a breath and fought to control the quiver in my voice. "I was in the process of searching the names in the *Observer* database. I found a match yesterday. A dancer by the name of Claire-Marie Renavand. She owns a small studio in town. I went to see her . . ."

"Dear God, Hayden!" Grandmother's voice filled the room. "You could have put yourself in grave danger!"

"Let her finish," said my father. "This may be helpful." He rarely spoke up against my grandmother, but I think his concern for Sapphire overrode his usual silence.

She nodded. "Proceed."

"The dancer became defensive and angry when I asked about her mother. She said she was obsessed with the ferry, youth, and beauty. She said her mother disappeared and left her penniless."

"Anything else?" Axel asked.

"No. She refused to speak to me after that."

"The Gladstone possibility," said Axel. "I'll call Jaxson. He may want to send someone over to question her." Axel turned his back to the room to make the call.

Everyone else returned their attention to their files.

"Hey. This is bizarre," said Cobalt. "I've found another entry with Emily Caldwell's signature. It also says '*Denied*'."

Cobalt had no idea how his words affected me. I pressed both hands to my stomach, closed my eyes, and sucked in a breath. I attempted to stay calm. My mother had tried to take the trip twice and was denied both times. I thought about Oliva's hint that she lived in Gladstone, but I didn't know if these attempted trips were recent or from years ago. My ears were ringing, but I saw Cobalt hand the page to Axel, who added it to the other page with the note about Gladstone.

Axel sat down and we went back to silent shuffling. I was doing my best to focus on the pages in front of me, but feelings of fear, anxiety, and regret were churning inside me. I pushed the feelings down and pressed my fingers to my temples as I forced myself to read the pages.

"Another one!" yelled Cobalt, as if he got Bingo in a game show. He waved the paper in the air. "Emily Caldwell. Denied."

I glanced over at my father. I'm sure he was thinking the same thing I was. Three attempts? Were these recent or old history? My mother disappeared when I was two days old, and neither of us had ever heard from her again. Could she possibly have gone to Gladstone? Could she be in Gladstone even now?

Cobalt added the page to the stack that was set aside. The shuffle of papers around me sounded loud in the quiet room.

"Found something!" yelled Omar. He stood

up. "A used receipt book. From the dry cleaner downtown. Used as scratch paper. Covered with names and numbers. And one copy has a date—from three weeks ago." He handed it to Axel, who was already dialing Jaxson.

Through the loud whooshing sound that filled my head, I heard Axel's voice as if from a distance.

"Possible location," he said. "Island Dry Cleaners. West Avenue. Meet you two blocks from there, corner of 34th."

While Axel was talking to Jaxson, my grandmother, always sharp in a crisis, began barking orders. "Cobalt and Omar. Go with Axel to meet the sheriff. The rest of us will continue to search the documents."

I stood up fast, knocking papers to the floor. "Grandmother, please! Let me go with them!"

Axel grabbed his keys off the counter. The men were rushing out the door.

"Please. I need to do this." I looked at her, my eyes wild with desperation.

My grandmother paused for barely a moment. Then she nodded briskly. "Go."

35

We arrived at West and 34th just as Sheriff Jaxson was getting out of his car. Another officer, whom I'd never met, climbed out the other side of the vehicle.

Jaxson pointed at the man. "Deputy Ryan." They were both wearing gun belts, which increased my anxiety level.

Another car pulled up behind us, and I worried that we'd been followed. That made no sense even as I thought it, but I was jumpy.

The driver leapt out of the car. It was Han. He was holding a gun and looking far too comfortable in the situation than an insurance investigator ever should. Even with one arm in a sling, he looked awfully healthy for someone recovering from a fall off a cliff.

"Let's move," said Jaxson.

Cobalt, Omar, Axel, and I followed behind Jaxson, Han, and the deputy. From this viewpoint, the street was empty. It was just getting dark and the streetlights were on. Unlike the usual cozy glow that I felt when I saw them, they appeared like evil, yellow eyes today.

We slowed to a crawl two stores away from the dry cleaners. The building appeared dark. As we got near, I could see the '*closed*' sign in the window.

Jax held up his hand to halt our movement, and he crept forward and peered in the window and checked the door, then returned to us.

"Door's locked. Lights are on in a back room. Ryan, Han, Axel, Omar, come with me around the back. Hayden, Cobalt, you two stay out front. Hide against the side corner and watch. Text if you see anything. Put your phones on silent."

I watched the men sneak around toward the back of the building. It was only minutes, but it felt like hours.

A car pulled up in front. One of the ferry mechanics stepped out. He was wearing jeans this time, but it was him. He was unmistakable. He was holding several large Subway sandwich bags. He bypassed the front door to the dry cleaner and used a key to open an unmarked door just beyond the entrance. As he went inside, I slipped over to the door and put my toe at the bottom, preventing it from shutting all the way and relocking.

Cobalt was right behind me. He whispered, "I texted Jax."

We looked at each other. I tipped my head toward the door and Cobalt nodded. I was thankful he was my watch partner, because none of the others would have agreed to follow the mechanic. But I was running on adrenaline and desperate to help Sapphire.

The door opened to a set of dark stairs. It appeared they went up to the apartment above the cleaners. We crept up, one silent stair at a time, until we were about halfway. We could hear voices and stopped to listen.

"Are we 'spose to feed her?" said a man's voice.

"Don't think so," answered a second. "We'd have to take the gag off. She could scream."

"She'll miss dinner."

"Yeah. But she'll be home by breakfast."

"And we'll be on a ferry. When this is over, I'm askin' for a big raise."

"Yeah. With the client list, they'll both be rollin' in the dough."

"Some of that dough ought to be ours."

"No kidding. I signed up for guard work, not to watch a murder."

"Man, that was horrible."

A third voice entered the conversation. I recognized that deep, gravelly voice. "What's so horrible about bashing someone over the head?"

"Are you kidding?" said the first. "The scream, the blood. Horrible."

"You idiot. That's 'sarcastic irony.' Remember what that means?"

"Ohhh. Yeah. Means the opposite. So even though you did it, you still thought it was horrible?"

"Shut up and eat your sandwich."

The deep voice sounded like Kerbie, the helmsman. It was possible that the third voice was the other mechanic.

I could not believe what I was hearing. This wasn't a possibility of danger. This was real danger. Cobalt held up his phone to show me that he had sent another text to Jaxson. We crept further up the stairs.

We remained still and quiet at the top of the landing. I was hyperventilating, so I tried to access my yoga breathing to keep it under control.

At that exact moment, the alarm beeped on my phone. A reminder to feed the cats their dinner. I fumbled to shut it off, but I wasn't fast enough.

Kerbie Gomez flung open the door, the two mechanics, Gronk and Shrek, right behind him. Kerbie grabbed my arm and yanked me into the room. The mechanics grabbed Cobalt.

Kerbie snatched my phone out of my hand and threw it on the floor. Then he stepped on it with the heel of his boot.

The mind was a funny thing sometimes. My immediate thought was that I was glad I had purchased phone insurance. Then I snapped back to the reality of the moment.

We were outnumbered—three enormous men against me and Cobalt. One man continued to hold Cobalt with his arms behind his back. The other two pushed me into a chair and secured my arms and legs with zip ties. Then they shoved Cobalt into another chair and tied his arms and legs to the chair.

"Where is Sapphire?" I shouted.

"Dammit. She's a screamer. Gag her," said

Kerbie.

The second man put a piece of duct tape over my mouth. Cobalt was sitting silently, watching.

Then the room was anything but silent.

The door slammed open. Jaxson, Axel, Ryan, Han, and Omar burst into the room. Three of them held guns, pointed. Omar and Axel were in a fighting stance, with fists up.

"Hands up!" yelled Jaxson. "Now! Hands up!"

The deputy came around behind them and secured all three with handcuffs, then instructed them to stand against the wall.

Han, Axel, and Omar began opening the doors to the other rooms.

"Found her!" yelled Han.

I was trying to turn my head to see inside the room where Han was yelling from. Jaxson had removed the tape from my mouth and was cutting the zip ties from my wrists and ankles. I got up and turned around just as Han was coming out of the room, with his uninjured arm—still gripping a gun—around Sapphire's shoulders. She looked frightened but appeared unhurt. She ran over to me. I stood up and enveloped her in a massive hug. Her body was shaking, and she started to cry.

The two mechanics were flustered. They were yelling at Kerbie.

"It's all your fault!" shouted one. "If you'd of

left the captain alive, we'd have found the box! We were close!"

"You're such a damn hothead!" hollered the second. "Bashing her ruined the whole plan!"

"And stealing the girl was stupid! Didn't you think they'd go crazy to find her? She's a Caldwell, you idiot!"

"You cost me my raise!" the first man howled.

The mechanics were too worked up to realize that they were throwing Kerbie under the bus. He realized it though.

"You two shut up!" bellowed Kerbie. He was turning as red as his hair.

36

I had finally completed the first issue of the paper. The story was so gripping that it was easy to sell ads to the local businesses. I was proud to release the first edition of the new online *Observer* so soon after taking over the job. Granted, it was just four pages long, and it was the only post on our new website, but the cover story was enough to carry the issue and launch the publication.

My camera had appeared around my neck after Sapphire's rescue, and I was able to snap some exceptional photos at the scene. One shot in particular—of Kerbie Gomez glaring at the camera—was perfect for the front page.

I couldn't help but read the story one more time.

Man Arrested for Ferry Captain's Murder Meets Dramatic End
by Hayden Caldwell

Ferry helmsman charged with murder of ship's captain dies in fiery car wreck

Kerbie Gomez, helmsman of the Destiny Falls Ferry, had been taken into custody and charged for the murder of the ferry captain that occurred one week prior. The body of Nakita Morozova Volkov, commonly known as Nakita Morozova, was found on the return voyage of the ferry by the cleaning crew. She is believed to have died of blunt force trauma to the head. A metal table leg found at the scene is suspected to be the murder weapon, according to the sheriff's report.

Gomez, a professional ferry helmsman, had worked in the DF Ferry system for five years. He had originally escaped notice because of his position on the staff and his apparent friendship with Morozova. It has since been revealed that the two were involved in an alleged illegal transport scheme, the sheriff's office said.

Morozova was in possession of top-secret vessel documents related to the scheme. It is believed that a argument occurred between her and Gomez over the material, a fight which led to her death. At the time of the argument, she had already shipped out the box of documents to an undisclosed location.

In an attempt to locate and steal the documents, Gomez hatched a kidnap and ransom plot. He and two other men, mechanics for the ferry system, Jared and Herman Serano, kidnapped a woman whose family was harboring the documents. They broke into the victim's home and left a note for the family, demanding the box of documents in exchange for the kidnap victim. They held the woman at the apartment above the downtown dry-cleaning shop run by Gomez.

Clues uncovered in the documents led

Sheriff Jaxson Redford and a team of investigators to the dry-cleaning shop, where the victim was rescued unharmed and Gomez apprehended. The name of the kidnap victim is being withheld at the request of the family.

Miranda Spencer, identified as Gomez's landlady, said that Gomez rented the two-story building, running the dry-cleaning business on the main floor and living in the apartment above. She'd had no complaints or issues with him. Spencer was shocked to learn that Gomez was not the proprietor that she thought she knew. "He always said hello and chatted with me. He'd been quiet, polite, and paid his rent on time," she said. She has been unable to reach other members of the Gomez family, and the dry-cleaning office remains closed.

Several members of the ferry staff had seen a different side to Gomez, calling him moody and a loner. He was known to spend time with the Serano brothers and the captain outside of work hours. The group kept to themselves and seldom socialized with any other members of the ferry staff or crew.

Statements made by the mechanics in exchange for plea bargains provided enough verifiable evidence to link Gomez to the crime. The Serano brothers claim little knowledge of details of the transport scheme, but verified that a criminal partnership between Morozova and Gomez existed. The combination of prior evidence plus their statements provided enough substantiation to place him under arrest for the murder of Morozova.

Sheriff Jaxson Redford took Gomez into custody at the time of the kidnapping, and he was held overnight at the Destiny Falls jail.

The morning following the arrest, Deputy James Ryan was transporting Gomez to the medium-security prison in Belfair Ridge when his squad car blew a tire, which spun the vehicle over the guardrail near the coastline. Ryan was able to exit the vehicle before it exploded and is recovering at Destiny Falls General Hospital. Gomez had been trapped in the back seat and perished in the flames.

The landlady and ferry staff have spoken to detectives and are cooperating with the investigation regarding the possible transport scheme. However, with the deaths of both Morozova and Gomez, a source tells us the investigation into the scheme has been stalled. It appears that the two criminals died taking untold secrets with them.

37

The Witch

The Jeannie-ized witch was painting her toenails pink when her doorbell pealed. It shocked her into spilling the pink goo all over her footstool. No one dared to sneak up on her! It was unheard of! If those idiot men had figured out a way to do so, she would make them pay for their error.

The doorbell rang again. Angered, she lifted her finger, poised and ready to punish them. She flung the door open.

The gale-force anger of her visitor flung her against the back wall of her cave. She stood there, rubbing the back of her head in shock. Her eyes grew wide with fear.

"You will stop. Now." The words echoed off the walls.

She had not heard her sister's voice in many years. But it immediately struck a chord of terror. Her sister might fool others with her fancy appearance. But the witch was not fooled. She knew the power her sister held.

The witch attempted an innocent look. "I don't know what you're talking about."

"Do not think me a fool, sister. I see right through your disguise to your heart. I have been watching you. Hoping your exile has been long enough to teach you a lesson. Father would be disappointed."

"Do not bring him up in my home," the witch growled.

"This home?" Her sister waved her hand around the room, and the genie bottle décor melted into the ground, leaving only the bare, ugly cave.

"Eh. I was tired of that ridiculous bottle anyway." She flipped her long, blond ponytail over her shoulder.

"Really sister? Jeannie the genie? You have always been so vain. Have you learned nothing? Perhaps returning to the ancient crone's body is necessary."

The witch looked down at her freshly-painted, pink toenails. She helplessly watched them change back into the old, gnarled feet she'd been forced to wear these past forty years. Ugh.

"Alright." Her shoulders sagged, and she scuffed her unpainted toes in the dirt. "What do you want of me?" she asked.

"You know what I want. Stop manipulating the citizens. Suffer your punishment as it was intended. Learn something. Perhaps you will find yourself liberated."

"In the meantime, what should I do?"

"Meditate? Read? Plant a garden? Write a book?"

The witched laughed at that. "Once upon a

time, in a dark and dreary cave . . ."

Her sister looked irritated, not amused.

The witch tapped her knobby fingers on her arm. "If I promise to be good, can I have something better than this bare cave to live in?" She tried to look innocent. It didn't work.

"Your promises have always been meaning-less."

Her sister sounded annoyed. She'd better try a different approach. "Something else, then. Penance?"

Silence was her answer. So, she waited. Counted in her head to a hundred. It had always worked before. Her sister was too kind-hearted, even though she pretended otherwise.

"Penance. Then you shall have an improved living space. Of my choosing."

"Pfff. Fine."

Her sister approached and held out her hands, palms up. "I will use the power of two. You can give back some joy where you have removed it."

"You know I hate that," the witch whined. Oh, she did. She hated that goodie-two-shoes stuff. But now that her sister had offered, she'd be a fool not to take it. She gingerly placed her hands upon her sister's.

The sister began to chant.

When the witch realized what she was doing, she recoiled, drawing her hands back.

Her sister glared. "You have only yourself to

blame for this. For once in your long, godawful life, do one kind thing for someone else."

The witch paused. "Ack. Fine. Perhaps it will count toward my redemption."

She replaced her hands as the words swirled in the air around them.

Then it was done, and her sister was gone.

The witch turned around in eager anticipation to see her new living space. She clutched the bodice of her old-fashioned dress and gasped.

It was an exact replica of their childhood home. From the year 1840.

38

"Good morning! Time to get up, Buttercup!"

I woke to the sweet voice of my cat. Meows from Chanel and little Lola followed, which I interpreted to be their good mornings too. I reached over and gave all three a morning rub.

"It's the ten-day-a-versary since Sapphire's dramatic rescue. Oooo, and nine days since Kerbie's demise. Or can I say death now?"

"I think you can stick to demise for now," I said.

The horror of the entire episode was still fresh in my mind. I was grateful that the family had accepted my sincere and repeated apologies for withholding the box from them. They understood the deep need to protect the family and realized that my intentions were pure. Misguided, they said, but pure.

I sat up and looked out the window at the sunrise. Hmmm. I could always watch the sunset from my room. Did the house revolve or did the sun? With Destiny Falls, one could never be sure.

"Guess what, Pussycat? The grand dame will be calling you down to her office this morning."

"Oh, boy. Does Chanel know why?" I asked. Because, of course, that's where she got her news.

Meeeow. Meowww. Meow. Meeeeow. Meow. I'd

never heard Chanel so talkative.

"Nope. No idea," said Latifa. But she wouldn't look me in the eye.

"Fine. Keep your secret. I'll find out soon enough." I slipped out of bed and did a few morning stretches.

My phone pinged.

Your grandmother requests your presence in her office at 7:00 a.m.

Good morning, Cleobella. Thank you. : -)

Good morning, dearest.

Then she added an emoji of a purple octopus. I assumed it was her version of a smiley face.

"Good morning, Grandmother." I walked into her office and planted a gentle kiss on her cheek. The fact that she turned her face up to accept it brought me a rush of happiness. Seeing a small, black kitten asleep on her lap made me smile.

"Take a seat, granddaughter."

Out of nowhere, Cleobella appeared and placed a cup of tea on the end table beside me. She put a fresh cup in front of my grandmother, then quietly exited the room.

I didn't notice what she was wearing. I was so apprehensive about the reason for my grandmother's summons, I was keeping my eyes on her, waiting for her to speak.

"Congratulations on your first *Observer* issue. The cover story has captured the attention of the entire community. Well done, my dear."

"Thank you."

"Are you able to continue with a monthly issue?" she asked.

"I'm sure that I can. The story opened doors for me. Everyone appears to be anxious to talk, which gives me a great opportunity to hear all the gossip."

"Shall we call it local commentary?" She looked amused.

Local commentary. I liked that. It fit my new image of the community newspaper editor. I could even use that name for a regular column.

Grandmother picked up her cup and sipped her tea. Was that it? Was that the reason for a meeting? She hadn't dismissed me, so there was more to come. I sat still and waited.

"I have worked with a friend to orchestrate a very special occasion for you. You may consider it a gift. A sign of my appreciation for your dedication to the family. You have embraced us all with your bungling, kind-hearted passion, and I wish to show my gratefulness."

Did she really have to include bungling? Hmm. I supposed it was accurate. The rest of her words settled in my heart with a joyful warmth.

"There are strict regulations and rules that you must unerringly adhere to, so I expect you to abide by these completely. There is no room for error."

"Yes. I'm listening."

She set her palms flat on the desk before her and leaned forward. "No. Do not merely listen. You must understand. It is critical." She stared deep into my eyes to convey the seriousness of her statement. I nodded.

"I have arranged for a visit from your grandmother, great-grandmother, and friend."

I stared at my grandmother. I was frozen. Her words echoed in my mind. My mouth could only hang open uselessly. No words escaped, only a sound. A gasp of confusion and bewilderment.

My grandmother patiently sipped her tea in silence, waiting for me to process what she had said.

"They're coming? Here?" I asked. The words themselves were understandable, the meaning behind them was almost too huge to comprehend.

She nodded. "It has been set for today."

"Today?"

Again, she nodded.

"But . . . They know nothing about Destiny Falls! What if they panic? What if they don't understand?"

"We have had several long conversations. You underestimate them, Hayden."

"You have spoken to Nana and Gran?"

"And to your friend, Luna. Yes."

"And they know? They understand?"

"As best they can."

I remembered how Luna ran screaming from the room. Of course, she had thought I was in danger. Once she realized I was safe, she'd embraced the bizarre situation that I found myself in.

"Are you ready to hear the conditions?" my grandmother asked.

"Yes, please."

"Rare and powerful magic will bring them here. It is not something to be trifled with."

She actually said the word 'magic.' I sat up taller in my chair and leaned forward, memorizing every word as she spoke.

"They will arrive at noon. They may not leave Caldwell Crest. Not one inch beyond the property borders. They will leave at midnight. Not one second beyond. If they aren't at the portal at the departure time, they will be snatched from wherever they are, but will not necessarily be returned to their home."

Grandmother paused and then repeated herself almost verbatim. "Do you understand?"

"I understand."

"Very well. I will meet you at the top of the stairs at quarter till the hour. They will require an hour or so of rest upon arrival. The guest room directly across from the stairs will be theirs for the day. You will have time for a private visit. We will all greet them in the gardens at family dinner tonight. After which I'll escort you all upstairs for your farewell."

She pursed her lips and looked at me over the top of her glasses. "That's all."

Then she smiled and winked at me. Very unlike Miranda Priestly.

39

I walked out of Grandmother's office like a lady. Then I turned around and ran back in. I embraced her in a tight hug and was pleased to feel her hug me back.

"Thank you," I whispered.

"My pleasure, granddaughter," she replied.

I left her office with a bounce to my step and ran up the stairs to my room. I picked up Latifa and spun her around the room.

"Woah, woah, woah. Slow down, Giggles. You're getting me dizzy."

"Oh, Latifa!!! Guess what? Nana, Granana, and Luna are coming for a visit! Today!" I spun her around again.

"Seriously, Bubbles. Stop with the spinning."

I plopped her down on the bed. *"So, she pulled it off, did she? That woman has some high-ranking friends, I tell ya."*

"I can't believe it! It's too much!" I pressed my palms to my cheeks, trying to reign in my excitement.

Chanel and Lola were on the floor, batting around a toy mouse. Latifa mewed to them, then Chanel came up and rubbed her head against my leg.

"*She's happy for you,*" said Latifa.

"Yes, I can see that. Thanks, Chanel." I stroked her beautiful, white fur and she purred. Little Lola was still spinning on the floor, fighting with the toy mouse.

"*Want some wardrobe assistance?*" Latifa asked.

"Oh, I don't need any help!" I laughed. "I could show up in a paper bag and the three of them wouldn't even notice. That's real love, you know. When someone sees your heart, not your outfit."

There was no slow meandering down the hallway today. I was race walking.

I was a few minutes early, but Grandmother was already there. She was seated on a bench beside a door just past the stairs. A mysterious door that hadn't been there in over a month. I recalled this door with a bit of a shiver. It had appeared once before. Jade had somehow arranged for an opening to the portal to try to send me home. But there was no way I could leave then. I never understood Jade's motivation and wasn't sure if it was even worth a moment of my memory. Especially today.

Grandmother stood up and opened the door. I followed her up the familiar stairs to the attic. It was exactly as I remembered. A clean and tidy attic filled with boxes and unused furniture. The centerpiece of the room was an antique dresser with a large mirror. A duplicate of the one

I had in my childhood bedroom. The one in which I'd had my first glimpse of Destiny Falls when I was six.

Grandmother sat at one of the upholstered chairs across from the dresser. She advised me to sit in the other chair.

"Please remain seated until our guests arrive," she said, as if we were waiting for friends to come over for tea. "It will prevent you from getting too close to the mirror and interfering with today's purpose." She looked at the time on her phone. "Just a few minutes now," she said.

Grandmother sat with her hands in her lap. A picture of elegance and patience. I sat beside her, a picture of nerves and excitement. I couldn't stop my legs from bouncing and I kept crossing, then uncrossing my arms. I stared at the mirror, seeing only the reflection of the attic.

Then the reflection began to change.

I looked in the mirror and saw Nana, Granana, and Luna standing there. They each had a rolling suitcase and a purse. Gran was wearing her traveling outfit—an ankle-length denim skirt and an embroidered denim jacket. She wore this ensemble for every flight or train ride I'd ever seen her take. The three of them were standing side by side, and I could just about feel their bubbling excitement.

A moment later, there was a brilliant flash of light from the mirror. And then they were standing in the attic, right in front of us, clutching each other from the dizzying trip through the portal.

Grandmother stepped forward in front of me and gave them each a glass of bubbling liquid. "Drink this," she said. "It will end the lightheadedness and speed your recovery from the transition."

They drank their tonics, then they rushed over to me. I was instantly wrapped in a group hug and surrounded by the ecstatic, laughing voices of my family.

Grandmother did an admirable job corralling us and getting us down the stairs and into the guest room. There was an abundance of chatter and energy. Then she respectfully left us to our reunion.

After a burst of excitement, the energy level in the room settled down to a vibrating hum. Luna and I were sitting cross-legged on the king-size bed. Nana and Gran had pulled up chairs beside us.

"I can't believe you're here! I've been wishing and dreaming of this moment since I arrived."

"How are you doing? Really?" Luna asked.

"Very well. This place feels like a part of me that's been missing. It's hard to explain. I'm so happy here."

Nana stood up and walked over to me. She gave me a hug and a kiss on the head. "That's all we ever want for you," she said.

I looked at Granana and she was nodding her head. "That's right, sweetie. Your happiness makes us happy."

They'd told me that all my life. Today I suddenly and totally understood what they were saying. Those weren't empty words. They were feelings deep in their hearts. My happiness mattered to them. It filled me with a sense of peace. If I stayed here, they would be okay with it.

Luna sighed a deep breath. "You know I want you happy, too. I just wish you could find your happiness where we could be together. I've missed you, friend."

"Me too."

There was a moment of quiet, then Luna wisely changed the subject. "Where's Sassy? Can we see her?"

"Oh! She's in my room. I'd like you to see that, too. And the gardens, you must see the gardens! But are you guys tired? Do you want a nap first?"

"Pshaw!" said Gran. "We can sleep when we get home! Lead the way, Hayden. We want to see everything."

Since we had less than a day together, I had asked Latifa if I could hold off telling them about my psychic communication with her. If I explained everything, I was afraid the day would disappear into a wild ride of disbelief and awe. She had reluctantly agreed, provided I told them her name was now Latifa.

We spent an hour in my room while they

exclaimed over the beauty of the décor and the setting. Gran instantly fell in love with my yoga room. Then the cats came out of their alcove and everyone oohed and aahed over the three felines. Afterwards, we strolled through all the gardens, sat by the koi pond, and talked and talked and talked. I filled them in on the Caldwell family, and who was who, and shared a few stories of my time here. It was wonderful.

I walked them to their room, where everyone was going to rest, change, and freshen up for the family dinner. Gran also wanted to put her feet up for a bit, and although I knew she wouldn't let on, I understood that a nap would give her an energy boost to get her through the rest of the day. I knew what would happen. She'd say, "I'm just going to put my head back and close my eyes for a bit." Then she'd snore for an hour and wake up energized.

I knocked on the guest room door and Luna flung it open and grabbed me in another emotional hug. She said she was getting her fill since it needed to last for a while. Neither of us addressed the fact that we had no idea how long that while would be.

"Wait until you see your gran. She's all dressed up for the family dinner."

"Oh, no," I said. "Did she pull out clothes from the back of her closet?"

Gran had a section in the very back of her

closet with all the party clothes from her entire adult life. She said she wore them so infrequently that they were 'just like brand new' and it was a waste to spend money on anything else. The problem being they were massively out of date and often sparkly.

I looked up to see her coming out of the bathroom all done up for the dinner. She was a sight. She had selected one of her favorite party outfits in honor of the special occasion. A Madonna-style get-up from the 1980s. She said that since she was in her eighties, it was the perfect choice. Typical Gran-style reasoning. Her tiny, not-quite-five-foot frame was nearly smothered in tulle, lace, necklaces, and bracelets. She was even wearing white, elbow-length, fingerless lace gloves. She had an enormous bow in her hair. On her feet were sparkly white sneakers. She explained that since the dinner was outside, they were sensible.

"Granana, you look very festive," I said, and gave her yet another hug. She beamed with delight.

Nana, Luna, and I all paled in comparison, but I thought we all looked beautiful.

We walked downstairs slowly while everyone enjoyed the beauty of the home. I was eager to see how the yard would be set up for this event. I wasn't disappointed.

The first thing I saw was a huge banner:

Welcome Granana, Nana, and Luna. It was strung between two trees festooned with balloons, and it had to be thirty feet across. The yard was bursting with blue and purple balloons, streamers, and twinkle lights. Blue was Nana's favorite color and purple was Gran's. I didn't know how they knew this, but Grandmother had her ways. A purple tent covered round tables set with festive place settings, and a blue tent covered several long tables arranged for a buffet dinner.

There was music coming from the speakers in the trees, playing instrumental Styx songs—Nana's favorite band.

The whole affair was festive and welcoming. I hugged myself and bit my lip to prevent an emotional breakdown. It was a blending of my two families, and it touched me deeply.

For the next hour, it was a blur of introductions and chatter. Nana and Gran were in heaven meeting all their new family members and hugging every one within an inch of their lives. I didn't know if I'd ever been so happy.

I realized that Gran had wandered away from us and I finally spotted her. Granana, in all her material-girl glory, was standing with Cleobella, dressed in her own sparkly party attire. The two of them were having a dramatic sign language conversation!

"Nana, since when does Gran know sign language?" I asked.

Nana looked over at her mother with pride. "Oh! She's been taking classes over at the senior center. I'm sure she's thrilled to be using her skills."

Luna was in her element—coming from a large family who gathered often, she felt immediately at home. I enjoyed introducing her to everyone, and they chatted with her as if she were an old friend.

I was standing with Nana when my father came over. I tensed in anticipation. She had not spoken to him since he disappeared on the day of my birth. Grandmother had explained that she'd told them the entire story. She had explained that Leonard had not left of his own accord and that he had suffered greatly from it. He approached us hesitantly.

Nana stepped forward and embraced him in a long, heartfelt hug. "Oh, Leonard. How you must have suffered." He embraced her in return. The two of them wandered off away from the group and sat on a bench near the gardens. She was holding his hand, and they were talking intently. I knew that feeling, having connected with him after a lifetime. It was beautiful to see.

Dinner was a lively event. The expansive buffet of food was amazing. The dessert table was filled with every possible choice of sweets, which Gran loved. I saw her with a plate covered from end to end. The family was warm and kind. It was more than I could have ever hoped for.

It was much too soon when I realized the evening was coming to a close. I gathered up Nana, Gran, and Luna. They said goodbye to the group, and there were hugs all around.

The four of us were subdued as we followed Grandmother upstairs to the guest room. She had said she would be back to escort us upstairs.

I sat in a daze while my little family gathered up their belongings. Gran removed her lace gloves and exchanged her fancy party clothes for her denim traveling outfit.

I was grateful for this time with them, I really, truly was. But now that it was nearly over, I felt a deep, overwhelming sadness wash over me. My stomach was in knots and I was finding it hard to swallow. The tears threatened, but I fought to keep them at bay. Sobbing hysterically would not be a good parting view.

Nana came to my side and gave me a kiss on the head and a hug. "This has been an amazing day, honey. It's been so good to see you, and lovely to meet the Caldwells. They are a wonderful bunch of people, and they seem to care deeply about you. I feel good about having you here with them."

"Thank you, Nana. I'm going to miss you so much." I wiped away a tear that had escaped.

Gran joined us. "You've got quite the family here, sweetie," she said. "They love you. I can tell."

Luna entered our little circle and took my

hands. "I'm happy for you, my friend. I'll miss you, but now I know where you are, so I can picture it. You keep sending those e-mails and texts. We'll video-chat through the mirror whenever it allows us."

I smiled at my friend's quick understanding of this odd place. "I'll work to set up more visits. I don't know how yet. But I will. I promise." I meant it too. It would be my goal to find a way to have regular visits with them.

There was a soft knock on the door. It was time. We walked down the hall and up the stairs to the attic, all holding each other. Grandmother followed at a respectful distance, allowing us our sorrow. No one spoke.

Finally, they stood in front of the mirror. Three of the most important people in my life. Pieces of my heart leaving me. I wanted to grab them away and tell them not to leave. I remembered Grandmother's warning. This was a mysterious, magical event, and they had no choice but to return at midnight, which was now.

A bright light flashed, and then they were gone. I collapsed into the chair and sobbed until I could barely breathe. Until there were no more tears left.

40

I entered my bedroom as quietly as possible, not wanting to disturb the sleeping cats. I wouldn't be able to talk to anyone right now, even Latifa. I crept into the closet and changed out of my party clothes, slipping into yoga pants and a tee. A session in my tranquil yoga room might help me find my center so I could sleep.

I spotted the box in the corner. Since the murder case was now closed, Jaxson had asked if I wanted it back, and I did. They had taken the originals of the lists of names and other documents pertinent to the ongoing investigation, and kindly left me copies. I thought I'd look through them now and find my mother's signatures. All the hellos and goodbyes of today were making me emotional, so I might as well add one more person to the hole in my heart.

I lugged the box into my yoga room. It was heavy, and I was weak tonight, so I dropped it on the floor. The bottom burst apart and papers scattered. I sat on the floor next to the mess. Well, how about that? There were more tears in me tonight.

Once I gathered my wits, I collected the papers and stacked them. Then I went out to my desk and retrieved a roll of packing tape.

I flipped the box over and noticed something odd. There was an envelope wedged in be-tween, where the cardboard had been folded over. I carefully removed it.

In my mother's distinctive, curvy, bold handwriting, a name was written on the envelope: *Hayden Caldwell.*

I stared at the envelope for a good, long while. I tried to control my breathing and heart rate. I had a premonition that opening this en-velope would change my life. How could it not? Finally, I carefully slipped my finger under the seal and opened it.

My darling daughter, Hayden,

I hope with all my heart that you find this letter. I have been trying in vain to reach you since you arrived in Destiny Falls. I have things I must tell you.

All your life you have believed that I aban-doned you. I want you to know that I did not leave you of my own choosing. You were my life, my precious new baby. First, I lost Leonard, the love of my life, gone so fast. So mysteriously he vanished. Taking with him my little son, my heart, my precious Axel. Then I was stolen from you. Not a day has passed that I don't grieve for you, for all that we've lost. Our little family, torn apart.

Your birth was a beacon. A beautiful thing, drawing evil to it. I discovered that it was the reason they found Leonard. They removed him to Destiny Falls. And it was the reason they found me. There are things you have never been told because no one knew the story to tell. I have learned much, and I will tell you some of these things now.

I have great pain and empathy for you being abandoned by your mother as a newborn. Because you see, they snatched me away from my mother, days after my own birth.

Days after I was born, I was found in Seattle, in unusual circumstances, too complicated to explain now. I was placed in a foster home with two wonderful, kind-hearted people who then adopted me. Your Nana and Granana. They did not know the circumstances of my abandonment, nor did they care. They embraced the maternal roles and raised me as their own. And then they raised you as well. They are saintly, beautiful women, and I miss them desperately.

It pains me to think they live with the belief that I left them willingly, without a backward glance. That I disappeared without a trace. Well, except for that horrible note that I was forced to write. The words cut me deeply and they created a scar on my heart that I feel to this day. "I can't do this. Take the baby. Goodbye." The smudges on that paper were remnants of my tears.

There are so many things that Nana and Gran did not know. Things that they could not know, for their safety and yours. Facts that were well hidden.

I was not a normal baby found in abnormal circumstances. Anything but normal. I didn't know my background until I was stolen away from you. That's when I began to learn the truth, in bits and

THE DISAPPEARANCE OF EMILY

pieces, over years of searching, prodding, and dis-covering one small piece at a time.

My mother brought me to Seattle. She had es-caped with me from a cold, dangerous island called Gladstone, which is where I was returned and where I remain.

There is one family here that holds a power within them: the Gladstones. It is a power that fuels the engine of Gladstone. They need the family here to maintain their illusions and their magic.

There is a parallel place where you find your-self now. Destiny Falls.

Gladstone and Destiny Falls are two halves of what was once a whole. The yin and the yang, the dark and light, the moon and sun. Destiny Falls is the posi-tive half, but it is also fed by the power of a family —the Caldwells. You father was needed there for that reason, as the Caldwell power runs through him.

Hayden, you need to know something very im-portant. My birth name was Emily Gladstone, and the Gladstone power runs through me. That makes you half Caldwell and half Gladstone. You are unique. I do not know exactly in what ways. I can only imagine what powers might flow through you. In all my stud-ies, I have not found there to be another like you.

I stopped reading and a thought hit me hard. What about Axel? He has the same bloodline as me. Why doesn't she talk about him? And what about my father? If she was still in love with him, wouldn't she address why she'd never reached out

279

to him? I was confused and overwhelmed. I sat on the floor in a daze and finished reading.

> *Keep this information well hidden. Do not tell anyone, as it can be used against you if the truth comes to light. I have learned in life that there is no one you can trust. Especially here. Be wise in this. Hold this information close. Memorize this letter and then destroy it.*
>
> *I will continue my attempts to reach you, but so far it has been hopeless. Please know that I love you with all my heart. Be careful, my sweet daughter. I hope to see you some day. Stay safe.*
>
> *Love, your mother, Emily*

~ ~ ~ ~ ~ ~ ~ ~ ~ ~

Thank you for reading!

I hope you've enjoyed your time in Destiny Falls. If you liked this book, please consider writing a review on Amazon, Goodreads, or another book site. Reviews are the best way to give a book life, and to say thank you to an author for a fun experience. Reviews are always appreciated!

Hayden's adventures in Destiny Falls continue in Book 3, when a mysterious old man shows up to tell her a series of tall tales. Who is he? And are his stories fiction? Or are they the history of her family, the islands, and the witch? Can he provide the information she needs to understand herself and her heritage, and possibly even free her mother? And why did a dead body show up . . . of someone who is already dead?

The Ghost Camper's Tall Tales Destiny Falls Mystery and Magic: 3

Stay informed about new releases.

Sign up for my mailing list here: https://www.nocrysolution.com/mailing-list/

Visit the series page at Amazon:

Learn more about the series here: https://www.amazon.com/dp/B08MCSN2KD

Printed in Great Britain
by Amazon